J574
H3

Hirsch

AUTHOR

Guardians of Tomorrow:Pioneers in
Ecology

TITLE

Ages:10 up

J574
H 3

2852

WHITEHAVEN METHODIST
CHURCH LIBRARY

Date Loaned

9-4-14			

Demco 38-295

Guardians of Tomorrow
Pioneers in Ecology

Also by S. Carl Hirsch

MAPMAKERS OF AMERICA
CITIES ARE PEOPLE
ON COURSE! *Navigating in Sea, Air, and Space*
PRINTING FROM A STONE: *The Story of Lithography*
THE LIVING COMMUNITY: *A Venture into Ecology*
FOURSCORE . . . AND MORE: *The Life Span of Man*
THIS IS AUTOMATION
THE GLOBE FOR THE SPACE AGE

Illustrated by William Steinel

S. Carl Hirsch

Guardians of Tomorrow

Pioneers in Ecology

The Viking Press / New York

Acknowledgment is made to Marie Rodell for permission to reprint selections from *Silent Spring* by Rachel Carson, Copyright © 1962 by Rachel L. Carson, published by Houghton Mifflin Company, and from "Of Man and the Stream of Time" by Rachel Carson, © Copyright 1962 by Rachel Carson, published by Scripps College, Claremont, California.

First Edition

Copyright © 1971 by S. Carl Hirsch
All rights reserved
First published in 1971 by The Viking Press, Inc.
625 Madison Avenue, New York, N.Y. 10022
Published simultaneously in Canada by
The Macmillan Company of Canada Limited

Library of Congress catalog card number: 76–136818

574.5   Ecology

Trade 670–35646–8   VLB 670–35647–6

Printed in U.S.A.

1   2   3   4   5   75   74   73   72   71

For my students in the "Man in Nature" class at Evanston Unitarian Church, whose deep concern for tomorrow's environment inspired this book.

Acknowledgments

A number of active "guardians of tomorrow" took time out from their efforts to save the environment to help me with the reading and revising of this manuscript. I want to thank: Raymond F. Dasmann, Senior Ecologist, Research and Planning, International Union for Conservation of Nature, Morges, Switzerland, and president of The Wildlife Society; William A. Niering, Professor of Botany, Connecticut College, and member of the Scientists' Committee for Quality Environment in Connecticut, and of the Ecological Society Study Committee to establish a National Institute of Ecology; George Marshall, conservationist; René Dubos, Professor in Rockefeller University's Department of Environmental Biomedicine, and member of Citizens' Committee on Environmental Quality; and Gaylord Nelson, U.S. Senator from Wisconsin.

I am also deeply indebted to Marie Rodell, literary agent and literary executor, Estate of Rachel Carson; to Granville B. Lloyd, Forest Service, U.S. Department of Agriculture; to Michael J. Walker, Fish and Wildlife Service, U.S. Department of the Interior; and to Paul L. Evans of the Tennessee Valley Authority.

Further, I want to acknowledge the gracious assistance of the Aldo Leopold family: Mrs. Aldo Leopold; Mrs. Marie Lord; Mr. and Mrs. Frederic Leopold; Professor A. Starker Leopold, School of Forestry and Conservation, University of California at Berkeley; A. Carl Leopold, Professor of Physiology of Horticultural Crops, Purdue University; and Edwin A. Hunger of Nogales, Arizona, boyhood friend of Aldo Leopold.

Finally, I offer a kiss of thanks to my wife, Stina, who was helpful on this project in more ways than I can name.

Contents

1. A Matter of Choice 14
2. Watcher in the Woods 24
3. The Hand of Man 38
4. The Country in the City 54
5. Thunder on the Mountain 74
6. Trees for Tomorrow 94
7. Troubled Waters 114
8. Lesson of the Land 138
9. Something in the Wind 154
10. Man the Choice Maker 168

Suggestions for Further Reading 179
Index 183

Guardians of Tomorrow
Pioneers in Ecology

A Matter of Choice

1. A Matter of Choice

And I brought you into a plentiful land to enjoy its fruits and good things. But when you came in you defiled my land, and made my heritage an abomination.

Jeremiah 2:7

America was deep into the stormy decade of "the '70s."

In the rain-washed streets of Philadelphia, early-morning crowds watched a young giant of a man stride toward the State House. The ruddy-cheeked outdoorsman, a rusty glint in his hair, was a lawyer from Virginia's western hills. "Thomas Jefferson," people whispered as he passed.

Philadelphians made a show of business as usual that Friday morning, June 28, 1776—acting as though they were unaware of the secret meeting in their midst. But the town hummed with high tension. All across colonial America, people waited anxiously while some fifty men debated the chances for life of a new nation.

In the Second Continental Congress, the arguments raged. Behind closed doors, a choice would be taken, a decision made. A feverish day passed, and then another, and several more.

Jefferson, stretched out loose-limbed in his chair, listened quietly to the debate. Occasionally he got to his feet to explain some part of the declaration which he had drafted, the meaning of phrases like the "inalienable rights" of Americans to "life, liberty, and the pursuit of happiness."

As young Jefferson spoke in clear, firm tones, he could hardly suppress his anger. A distant tyrant had taken from American colonists their right of free will. The British monarch allowed his subjects little say in running their own lives or in dealing with the destiny of their country. The time had come to declare the people's independence!

It was late in the afternoon on the fourth day of July, and the chairman pounded his gavel. In the white-paneled room, the delegates soberly voted "Aye!" for separation, Jefferson among them.

The young delegate from Virginia, his heart hammering in the drama of the moment, was elated. The momentous choice was made—leading to countless other choices which Americans could now make in determining the future of their own independent nation.

Signs of trouble

It was almost dusk when Jefferson stepped into the cobbled street, blinking in the last red rays of the lowered sun. His lodgings were in the modest home of a bricklayer, and he took the long way around, walking off the strain of the day.

Philadelphians were hurrying home from market, swatting flies, drinking in the taverns, shoeing horses, sweeping their front stoops. The news of the Congress's action would not be announced for several days.

Through Jefferson's mind raced thoughts of the crises just ahead. A military struggle was to be fought—and won. Yet to be determined was the form of the new government. A thousand matters of union, finance, foreign policy, war, and peace would have to be settled.

The Virginian was vaguely aware of other choices which must be made as well. Taking charge of a land so broad, so richly inlaid with resources, was no small venture.

What guarantees were there that the land would be safeguarded? Would its new rulers, the people, keep this country wholesome and healthy, pleasant and unspoiled—as it had been through all the centuries of the Indian past?

Founding Father Thomas Jefferson looked at the new republic, only hours old, and behold! it was good. A nation's tomorrow shone in his eyes. The United States, newborn, had the free, fresh look of the very young. To the Virginian, the country's future was bright with promise—even though, at times, he might notice some small disturbing signs. . . .

As he strolled, the young lawyer suddenly came upon some

men who were hewing trees, stately flowering chestnuts. Why, Jefferson wanted to know, were these handsome shade trees being destroyed?

The workmen gave him the answer. The insurance companies considered trees to be fire hazards and would insure no house with a tree in front of it!

At the river front, the walker paused. Carts were lined up at the water's edge, dumping sewage and waste matter into the stream. Except for a few private wells, the river was Philadelphia's main source of drinking water.

The lanky young statesman soon came to a district crowded with ugly structures. Here the poor of Philadelphia lived in utter squalor. The ramshackle buildings overflowed with filth. Barnyard animals roamed about. Drinking water trickled from a rusty pipe.

The streets were jammed with horse-drawn vehicles in a tangle of traffic. Overhead the sky was filled with black coal smoke pouring from the chimneys of mills and workshops.

In the gloom the statesman could see working people straggling out of factories at the end of their long day. Many of them were women, carrying dinner pails—and tiny children, their faces sooty and drawn.

This too was Philadelphia, Jefferson thought grimly to himself, the leading city of colonial America. And these were a few signs of its progress and prosperity.

Unanswered questions

By the time Jefferson became president of the United States, a new century had dawned. In his inaugural speech he listed the glorious merits of "a rising nation, spread over a wide and fruitful land."

"With all these blessings," asked Jefferson, "what more is necessary to make us a happy and prosperous people?"

The third president saw his nation laid out like a homemade quilt, strongly patterned from bits and pieces. America was a patchwork of farm lands, growing towns, and peaceful villages.

He realized that some men were grasping for power and wealth. And he was wary of those who might abuse the country, its resources and the people, for private gain. But he believed strongly in a form of government that gave the final choices to the common man—grain grower and greengrocer, printer and teamster, baker and bookkeeper, mason and tinker, weaver and wheelwright. Jefferson had great faith in the plain folk and felt the country to be secure in their hands.

True, the Virginian had just come from a drawn-out and bitter struggle. The actual skirmishes were fought over pieces of legislation, government policies. But the president had forebodings of bigger, more long-range issues at stake. It was "either-or":

A highly industrial America, driving headlong into a machine age, or a serene and comfortable land, its people earning a modest livelihood from its farms and workshops?

A government thrusting ahead to become a far-flung world power enmeshed in foreign rivalries, or a homebody neighbor, minding its own affairs, on friendly terms with everyone?

A people jammed into large, teeming factory cities, or a population spread out on the green landscape in a natural setting?

A country run by mighty commercial and banking interests, or a true democracy where the real power rests in the hands of small producers in family-sized farms and owner-operated shops?

A nation boasting vast quantities of products, or a community of citizens, proud of the quality of their lives?

In the ongoing struggle over deepening differences, Jefferson and his friends had won a few battles. But although it was he and not his opponents who now sat in the half-finished White House, the questions were still unsettled.

These would, in fact, be slow, silent decisions, made without fanfare or fireworks. The big choices would flow from America's values. People would reach deeply into themselves and find out what they wanted most, what they held dear. Hopefully, they would pick and choose what they considered to be the real needs of a good life, or "progress," or "the pursuit of happiness." And the long-range effects of these decisions might emerge so gradually that the change would be almost imperceptible.

A land transformed

Almost two hundred years had passed since the nation's founding. Suddenly Americans were startled by what had happened to their country. Their nation had become the mightiest of world powers, and the richest. But alongside that fact were some sober truths to deal with.

In the space of two centuries, Jefferson's America had drastically changed. A hideous blight appeared all across what the Virginian had called "the immensity of land." The future seemed in danger. The nation's ability to cope with the problems was in doubt. The wholesomeness and purity were gone.

"The Ohio is the most beautiful river on earth," Jefferson once wrote, "its current gentle, its waters clear." This great river, two centuries later, was edged by a hundred industrial cities, each pouring into it tons of waste and filth, so that in places its burden of greasy sludge was considered a fire hazard.

The clear skies that Jefferson once admired over his native land had vanished from all the centers of population—and even the desert winds, the mountain air, and the prairie breezes carried perilous foreign substances.

Whereas Jefferson once saw an urgent need for more population to fill up an empty land, the sheer numbers of people had become a threat.

In the West, where Jefferson had envisioned wildlife few men had ever seen, the wildest thing that appeared was man himself. He destroyed forests older than civilization. In the chaos of habitats which he created, deadly fumes poisoned the air. Periodically the fish and wildfowl along the ocean fronts were smothered in oil. Across the midlands, vast acres of fertile soil vanished in "black blizzards" of dust and in avalanches of silt river-borne to the sea.

Instead of Jefferson's vision of a rural America, placid and slow-paced, the nation had gambled on high-powered, high-speed, high-quantity production—with some dismaying results. Even imaginative Jefferson could not have dreamed of the mountains that appeared throughout his beloved land—towering peaks of junk and garbage!

Every small and large power source polluted the earth—and pollution was everywhere. One after another, the rivers turned sour and stinking. Over the cities the sun was seen dimly through a dark pall. Shores were littered with the dead bodies of fish, the beaches fenced off and forbidden.

More ominous were the scenes in hospitals, where men and women died of a mysterious cause that could only be described as "the environment." A new generation of children appeared, carrying in their organs and bones strange new chemical substances, the future effects of which were largely unkown.

The sickness that gripped America hardly had a name. Or else the name of it went unwhispered—like some plague of the Middle Ages.

Some of the most learned scientists questioned whether America could survive without revising completely its dangerous style of life. Others reached the sober conclusion that the entire planet, home of the human race, had been damaged beyond hope.

Sentinels on the land

In the 1770s, men and women had dreamed of pursuing happiness in a bountiful land. By the 1970s, Americans had utterly conquered the natural environment—and learned in horror that they had unwittingly destroyed part of themselves.

What had happened? How did America blunder its way to this condition? Somewhere along the way, did the nation take a wrong fork in the road, make a bad choice?

Maybe we should have foreseen that our "progress" was not what it seemed to be. Or perhaps sentinels should have been stationed across America, ready to cry "Beware!" wherever the land was being misused.

Strangely, such guardians did arise. They volunteered their services in every decade. Quietly, tirelessly, they watched—and warned.

Unbidden, they came forward on their own—like that odd New Englander, Thoreau. He appeared in historic Concord, caring deeply about the living environment, describing himself as its "self-appointed inspector."

Henry David Thoreau

Watcher in the Woods

2. Watcher in the Woods

> *To find the air and water exhilarating; to be refreshed by a morning walk or an evening saunter; to find a quest of wild berries more satisfying than a gift of tropic fruit; to be thrilled by the stars at night; to be elated over a bird's nest or a wildflower in spring—these are some of the rewards of the simple life.*
>
> John Burroughs

The day began with the boom of cannon. At each blast, the little girls screamed and the boys held their ears.

It was April 19, 1825—and the Massachusetts town of Concord was celebrating its part in the American Revolution, begun just fifty years earlier.

It would be a day filled with band music and rolling oratory, picnics on the green and dancing to the fiddle. The day would end with a torchlight parade and fireworks exploding against the spring sky. A few aged veterans of the War of Independence squeezed into their old uniforms. Down by the bridge they re-enacted in a pageant how they had surprised the redcoats and fired "the shot heard 'round the world."

Through it all, an eight-year-old boy watched in wonder. He skirted the edge of the crowd, marched for a time to the drumbeat of the parade. But soon he was off toward the woods. Perhaps he was drawn by a different rhythm—the rat-tat-tat of a nest-building woodpecker, the shrill chirping of spring peepers, or the tempo of trout passing silently in the shaded deeps of the stream.

He was christened David Henry Thoreau. "Contrary," people called him. And just to prove it he reversed the order of his given names to make it Henry David.

Even at an early age, he was as casual and cocksure as a little rooster. Henry exasperated his family and teachers by insisting that there be a very good reason for everything he was asked to do. The boy was a stickler for plain truth.

When a schoolmate accused him of stealing his knife, Henry merely replied, "I didn't take it," adding not another word. Later the real thief was found out. And Henry shrugged off an apology with, "I told you, I didn't take it."

The Thoreau family was poor, and the boy learned to separate the true needs of everyday life from false ones. Henry was so pleased with a new pair of boots that he wore them to bed!

He could be as prickly as a porcupine and as ill-mannered as a bluejay. His moods covered a wide range. Often he was somber and thoughtful. But on occasion Henry sang out the old ballads with gusto, danced impulsively out of sheer good spirits, or played his flute in the still night.

In later life he would recall his childhood, remembering, "My life was ecstasy." At first glance the drowsy New England village, surrounded by woods and streams, did not strike even its residents as being a very special place in which to grow up. But Henry caught a sense of rich beauty in this simple setting. He found adventure in everyday scenes. And whatever deep, clear spring of bubbling life he discovered in the forest, he kept pretty much to himself—until he was ready to speak out.

Somehow, Concord in those years had become a gathering place for some of the most gifted writers, artists, philosophers of New England. And often young Thoreau sat in their circle, shaping his own thinking in the midst of the lively conversation.

But he might just as readily escape toward the countryside.

With his older brother, John, he loaded a homemade boat with a few supplies and set off on a river cruise. Or else he took off with a friend on a beeline hike, walking steadfastly toward a distant peak, hurdling all obstacles. Once they walked straight through a house while the astonished farm family sat at dinner!

An odd fellow

The Concord citizenry were a hard-working people to whom nature was a bitter enemy. They struggled to make the soil produce, kept a wary eye on the weather, and saw the hills, forests, and streams mostly in terms of problems to be overcome. Success for them was measured by the size of their crops and the extent of their farm holdings.

In that society, Thoreau was a misfit. He taught in the town's public schools—only to be branded a failure because he refused to flog his pupils. As a surveyor he found that measuring out a wilderness area was too often the groundwork for its destruction.

Even his first effort at having a book published was a failure. The book, a tale of a river journey which he took with his brother, found no publisher who would risk the cost of issuing it. Finally Henry agreed to publish the book at his own expense.

Out of a printing of a thousand copies, only a few hundred were sold. One day a huge box arrived containing the unsold copies. Henry strained to drag the load up to his garret room, where he arranged the books on his shelves. "I have now a library of nearly nine hundred volumes," he wrote ruefully to a friend, "over seven hundred of which I wrote myself."

Behind his back, the villagers chuckled at Henry David Thoreau and his queer notions. He appeared to them to live among air castles and soap bubbles—an impractical, improvident dreamer. Or was he? Some things he said sounded strange, but if you thought about them a bit, they made a lot of sense.

His fellow townsmen saw Henry out of the corners of their

eyes passing across the fields, working occasionally at odd jobs, staring at a circling hawk, tramping through the deep snow.

Henry was peculiar—in the frank opinion of the town. He was a college graduate with no profession or career. Although far from lazy, young Thoreau seldom worked at a paying job. A fellow of brisk energy, spicy spirit, and sharp wit, to his Concord neighbors Henry seemed somehow to lack ambitions and goals.

Clean-shaven and neatly dressed, he had a woodsy appearance, blending with the foliage like a tree toad. His dark hair looked as though it had been combed with a pine cone, and in summer his skin took on the sun-browned color of a walnut. In the countryside he carried a whittled stick, more for poking around than for aid in walking.

An inquiring pair of deep-set gray eyes searched out happenings within the landscape that few men would have noticed. Henry was witness to the construction of woodland dwellings— the nests of paper wasps, cobwebs, and the wet, untidy abodes of muskrats. He kept appointments to attend the comings-out of tadpoles and skunk cabbage, the arrivals of bluebirds and high-flying geese. He found himself one day flapping his elbows, goose-fashion, and sounding a wild cry in a vain effort to draw down to earth a northbound flight of migrants.

To him the spring was summed up in the pungent smell of the witch-hazel blossom. And fall was celebrated with a moonlight stroll, listening to the hooting of owls, swishing the dry leaves underfoot, "walking in night up to your chin."

A sense of beauty

Although Thoreau had a great deal of business with wild plants and animals, the species that interested him most was man. He spent much of his time at lecturing and even more at writing. A friend said that Henry had chosen for himself the special task of depicting for his fellow man "those yet unspoiled

American things, and of inspiring us with a sense of their homelier beauties."

This was an age of eloquent, grand-mannered orators—and Thoreau was not one of them. His speaking style was as artless as a friendly chat. He was not tall and had short arms, a prominent nose, and well-worn clothes. Appearing on the local lecture platforms around the state, he was not a very popular speaker and earned very little in fees.

Thoreau's writings and speeches dealt mainly with the common things that he observed in nature. There was nothing sensational about his wilderness experiences, no hair-raising adventures or harrowing hardships, no far-ranging journeys or extraordinary discoveries.

And yet he wove a rich cloth out of familiar, everyday materials. He wrote superbly about nearby places, blending the colors and textures of every season into harmonious patterns. Through it all ran the design of Thoreau's wandering thoughts about man interwoven with the natural environment.

Thoreau's writings would someday make up twenty brilliant volumes. Little of it ever saw the light in his own time, remaining buried in his rambling journals, to which he added almost daily.

But little by little, his sense of nature's beauty reached out to those around him. The children of Concord found in Thoreau an exciting companion. To walk in the woods with Henry was an adventure, a treasure hunt. He knew where to find the hidden lairs of foxes and how to make music by blowing on a blade of grass. A fascinating day might be spent with him just watching a wild duck teach its newly hatched young the secrets of the river.

Slowly the townsfolk made Thoreau one of their own. They didn't pretend to understand him or to agree with many of his views. But in small ways they showed him they were aware of what he was trying to say.

A villager led him to where a bittern was nesting. From a farm woman he received some rare wild flowers. A neighbor asked Henry about an albino bobolink. And a farmer confessed to him his deep enjoyment of a misty scene across the marsh. In turn, Thoreau gave them all some idea of what to look for if they really wanted to enrich their lives.

However, even in little Concord, this was a booming era of mechanical wonders and the promise of plenty in newfangled machines. Clearly, a nation of glory-bound people would not turn its back on abundance—and follow Thoreau out into the wilderness. Nor did it even stop to consider that choice.

A style for living

If Jefferson was the designer of American liberty, Thoreau was one model of how to live it. Early in life, Henry boldly declared his own independence. He set himself free from the need to accumulate money or "things," preferring instead to devote himself intensively to what he called living.

He was a free-moving wayfarer in the byways of his homeland. His days were spent in observing, thinking, writing, showing concern for everything in the living community. Thoreau was a walker, and his easygoing pace was just right for sightseeing. He took the least-traveled roads. When Henry said he was "going by rail," he usually meant walking along the train tracks.

He and a friend discussed a trip to Fitchburg one morning. The conversation went like this:

FRIEND: Let's take the train; we'll certainly get there faster.
HENRY: No, I think we'll go faster afoot.
FRIEND: Now, Henry, you're not making any sense.
HENRY: Suppose we try it out and see who gets there first.
FRIEND: Look here, I just don't understand you.
HENRY: Well, now, let's see. If I leave here this morning, I can walk to Fitchburg by tonight.
FRIEND: Yes, that's right.

HENRY: And if you go by railroad, you will have to pay the fare, and how much is that?

FRIEND: Oh, about a day's wage, I guess.

HENRY: That means you will have to work today in order to earn the fare—and you won't get to Fitchburg until tomorrow!

FRIEND (reluctantly): Yes, I see what you mean.

One thing Thoreau knew for certain. A man's time on earth was not meant to be spent in continuous drudgery, grubbing ceaselessly toward goals that brought him no real happiness or fulfillment. He saw his lifetime as a precious possession. He knew that he had to exchange some part of it for money or goods—but he was determined to trade away as little as possible.

All around him, he saw people giving up their lives in order to build a mound of belongings. Most of this was pointless clutter— "hindrances," said Thoreau, to the real business of living. His neighbors toiled at such mound building six days of the week, resting on the seventh so that they could go back to the endless routine.

The order of things should be reversed, Thoreau believed— work for one day to earn the real necessities of life, and live during the other six! "If I should sell both my forenoons and afternoons," he wrote in his journal, "I am sure that for me there would be nothing left worth living for."

But was it really possible to reorder one's existence, to eliminate the bric-a-brac and gimcracks—and to concentrate simply on exploring the grandeur of oneself and the surrounding world?

A rich, simple life

Henry built a hut for himself just outside of town. And here he lived by the wooded shore of Walden Pond, whose clear waters he drank from a dipper. With homemade furniture, a few utensils, and a small vegetable patch, he spent two years. He lived "gloriously" on a few cents a day.

He was not a hermit. He made trips into town and worked occasionally in the community as a handyman, surveyor, farm hand. His cabin was visited by friends and townsfolk, by the envious and the curious. At the same time Henry had ample solitude, time to think for himself, to be creative, "to learn what life teaches." A friend called Henry's cabin "a sentry box on the shore."

His period at Walden Pond was for Thoreau an experiment in how to live simply and yet fully. He found proof that a man really needs very little in order to live in comfort. In those two years Thoreau learned the lesson of his lifetime. No longer was there any chance, he said, that "when I came to die, I would discover that I had not lived."

One autumn evening he was in his cabin writing in his journal, recording his observations of the environment:

> I sit here at my window and observe the phenomena of three thousand years ago, yet unimpaired.
>
> The tantivy of wild pigeons, an ancient race of birds, gives a voice to the air, flying by twos and threes athwart my view or perching restless on the white pine boughs occasionally; a fish hawk dimples the glassy surface of the pond and brings up a fish; and for the last half-hour I have heard the rattle of railroad cars. . . .

Changes in the landscape

The train that invaded the shores of Walden Pond changed Thoreau's quiet world almost overnight. Roaring through the landscape came a new age of power and speed, commerce and industry. By mid-century all of New England was a web of rails. The 1850s saw trainloads of farm produce, lumber, and manufactured goods being hauled cross-country.

New factories were being built with frightening speed. Eager for profits, the owners started them running even before they were completely finished. Adequate housing, sanitation, safety measures—these were often promised, but lacking. The owners were now too intent on getting rich to bother with costly "frills."

The Massachusetts river towns were vibrant with the steady throb of machines. In Chicopee and Nashua, Holyoke and Lawrence, Thoreau heard the factory whistles howl across the countryside. At Lowell, farm-bred girls were awakened in company barracks at 4:30 A.M. by the clanging of a bell. Beginning their long day in darkness, they worked until after nightfall, tending the whirling cotton spindles. Tons of mass-produced goods were being made by the new industries. Most important of all, they were manufacturing a new environment for America.

The factories gave an altered appearance to the communities where they were built. The flood of factory-made products had a startling effect on the lives of people throughout this land. Most striking of all was the new routine of living for the millions who became the wage workers of the machine age.

Henry David Thoreau recognized that men needed to improve

the way they produced goods—and he welcomed the new methods, which saved time and energy. But it seemed to him that the new technology could be carried on without the evils of the factory system.

Henry was appalled at the toll of industrial deaths and illnesses. Mine disasters, factory accidents, the hazards on the railroads—all these filled him with sadness. The day would come, Thoreau remarked bitterly, when instead of being sent to prison, criminals would be put to work on the railroads as punishment!

Of all the turning mills invented by the new era of mechanical power, to Henry the worst of all was the treadmill of factory routine. It seemed to him that the factory system violated the very nature of man, reducing him to something as inhuman as the machine.

It troubled the Concord naturalist that men, women, and children were confined throughout the long day behind the walls of a wretched factory—to an existence devoid of joy or beauty. Men seemed recklessly to be doing violence to themselves, and to the surrounding natural environment as well.

By 1853, Thoreau had sensed that new and destructive forces were at work. In the country towns he knew so well, strange and explosive pressures were building up. Henry felt the tension growing as village life became regulated by the factory whistle and the time clock.

A new breed of industrialist had appeared, ruthless and single-minded. He was the absentee owner of enterprises located in communities where he did not live and of which he was not a part. He was after large profits, acquired as speedily as possible. It mattered little to him whether he made a "killing" at operating a shoe factory, at sending miners underground, or at cutting down a forest. The get-rich-quick operator presented himself as a new type of American hero.

Thoreau was not impressed. "If a man walk in the woods for love of them half of each day, he is in danger of being regarded as a loafer," Henry noted, "but if he spends his whole day as a speculator, shearing off those woods and making earth bald before her time, he is esteemed an industrious and enterprising citizen."

Thoreau's nightmare was a landscape tamed and crushed by the inroads of industry. In despair, he saw the natural scene going bad before his eyes. He needed no count of wild pigeons to see that their numbers were declining year by year. The fish were being killed off by wastes and sewage from the industry growing up along the river banks. Otters were now rare. The familiar trees with which Thoreau had grown up were vanishing.

"Every larger tree which I knew and admired," he recorded in his diary, "is gradually being culled out and carried to the mill."

A *cockcrow*

A rooster awakened Henry in the dawn of January 7, 1853, a perfect winter morning. Braced by the wind, his mind and body tense in the sharp, crisp cold, Henry made his early rounds. Walden Pond had frozen over during the night. He walked the shore line peering at the fish life through the dark, transparent ice. Stretched out full-length, he looked in fascination at a shining scene of great beauty below, where perfect spheres were formed by air bubbles frozen into the ice.

The naturalist greeted children going to school, picked up a few fallen nuts, checked the catkins on the birches for early signs of spring, and made his leisurely way home.

Just a little before 10:00 A.M., he was jolted by a powerful explosion that rocked the Concord countryside. For a moment the house shuddered and loose articles danced crazily on the shelves.

Thoreau raced wildly from the house. Northward, a low horizontal cloud had formed over the distant gunpowder factory. The main road, when Henry reached it, was a snarl of traffic. He jumped aboard a wagon, and soon he was at a scene of frightful disaster. The main building of the American Company's powder mill was a scorched, smoldering ruin. Heavy timbers and machinery had been flung far and wide by the blast. Shreds of clothing hung like strange fruit on the bare trees. Far out on the landscape, bits of wreckage lay charred and smoking in the snow.

For an instant it seemed to Thoreau as though fragments of the tragedy had been sown like seeds across the countryside. Henry brooded among the embers, stunned by grisly glimpses of bodies mangled and blackened.

"There is an avenging power in nature," Thoreau thought to himself. "Man, tampering with elements he understands only vaguely, touches off his own destruction."

Henry returned home pale with anger and heartsick. He scrawled in his journal a terse account of the factory explosion.

The naturalist tried vainly to resume his placid and gentle way of life. But he could not readily go back to snowbirds and ice crystals, to sauntering in the nut-brown woods and star-finding in the winter night. His mind would not shake loose the visions of torn lives and a shattered landscape.

The Concord naturalist often remarked that he was born in the nick of time. There were moments, however, when he felt he was all too late. Suddenly the encircling world seemed to be turning violent and dangerous. And Henry Thoreau felt some deep need to express his sense of anguish and foreboding. What could he say that would bring men to their senses? How best could he cry "Havoc!"?

That week Henry went to work on a final version of his book, *Walden*. It was to be, he said, a "cockcrow," a rousing cry for men to awake, to take a look at themselves and their world.

Northward in Vermont, another New Englander named George Perkins Marsh pondered the struggle of man and nature. For Marsh, an event in that stormy clash was the most vivid memory of his childhood.

George Perkins Marsh

The Hand of Man

3. The Hand of Man

It is not now as it hath been of yore—
Turn wheresoe'er I may,
By night or day,
The things which I have seen I now can see no more.
                                William Wordsworth

In the stormy night, the boy lifted himself, dripping, from a deep mudhole and made his way painfully along the riverbank. With each swift flare of lightning he took in a quick view of the awful scene.

Stumbling and sliding, George groped his way toward the bridge. After days of steady downpour, the rain was being driven by a high wind. But what filled the boy with dread was the strange, wild roar from the river below.

George glimpsed a dozen barrels bobbing in the torrent along with other debris of all kinds. Spreading over the protecting stone wall, the flood was seeping into his father's sawmill. With his poor eyesight, it seemed to him that the water had covered the whole countryside as well as the sleeping village on the far bank.

Suddenly the rolling echo of thunder filled the valley. Within seconds came another deafening crash. In the next flash of light, George could see that the bridge had collapsed! In horror, the boy caught sight of the massive trestle being carried off by the current. Torn beams hung from the riverbank.

"Father!" the boy screamed into the night. Up the slope he scrambled, fighting his way through the vines and brush. He was soaked and mud-covered. His spectacles had long since vanished. He made his way by feel through the blackness toward the big house up on the hill.

"Father!" His cries rang out above the storm. Pausing for breath, he gave one more piercing shriek. By the time he reached the terrace of the house, there were lights inside.

In moments, the boy gushed out his story of terror and ruin. Hastily men grabbed shovels and axes and rushed out into the night. Little George, wet and dirty, rested in his mother's arms, sobbing softly.

Collector of facts

That night of danger and alarm passed like a bad dream. Some urge had sent a small boy out into the storm, some need to see for himself how high the river had risen, how threatened were the wharves, mills, and bridges.

But George Perkins Marsh would again in his lifetime cry out a clear warning call. He seemed destined to be a guardian against deadly peril, a vigilant watcher in the murky night.

There was, in fact, a kind of storm brewing over America, signaled in Marsh's years by a cloud no bigger than his hand. But the Vermonter would sound his alert. And if the nation failed to heed it there would be a reckoning.

He was ten years old in that year of 1811, living in the town of Woodstock, in the great bend of the Ottauquechee River. George was the son of a New England country squire, a sickly boy whose childhood was one long struggle for survival.

Some unknown disease had dimmed his eyesight and turned his world into a misty blur. But he would not give up his books, and he squinted at the pages, impressing the words on his memory. It was a precious victory to get his mother or his older brothers and sisters to read to him. An encyclopedia, crammed with information, was his favorite reading.

As some boys play endlessly with toy soldiers, George Marsh paraded his facts. He gathered them in great numbers. He sent them, arrayed and marshaled, into battle against each other.

He was an unusual youngster, with a soft, owlish face, blinking through thick eyeglasses. Too gentle for boyish horseplay, he shied away from rough games. Though a schoolmaster's delight, George was a brainy bore to his classmates. A single question would unloose from the boy a rambling discourse on life in ancient Persia, or the workings of a steam engine, or the varied species of Vermont butterflies. His schoolmates taunted him with a dozen nicknames, all meaning "Sissy!"

George retreated to his books and to the solitude of "his" mountain. His father's property reached far up the slope of Mount Tom. And the boy climbed to a favored hideaway near the summit. Here he had a maplike view of the river and the village, the town square and the common.

Below him appeared a self-contained world, locked in the deep valley. The setting gave shape to the lives of its inhabitants, and it seemed to influence their character as well. These Vermonters were somehow free-spirited as the turbulent river, unyielding as the granite hills, stolid as the native hemlocks. These surroundings were for them a total environment that affected their everyday existence. George Marsh was also aware of the fact that the people, in turn, changed their environment.

A view from the heights

Woodstock depended heavily on its river, as did so many other New England towns. The river meant many things—water supply and shipping, ice cutting in winter and fishing in summer. In those days the stream was used to carry off waste of every kind. The idea of water pollution had scarcely occurred to anyone.

Increasingly, the river was the source of power. A village usually had its groaning water wheel, or a dozen of them. The wheel turned the gristmill or sawmill. As factories appeared, the river powered lathes and looms.

A special feature of New England towns was the "common" or green. This was a stretch of meadow owned jointly by the citizenry. The Woodstock green, where George Marsh flew his kite, was a grassy oval just off the town square.

The common served many public uses. In the early days each householder pastured his cows there. But the common typically became, in time, a hotly contested arena.

If a citizen grazed three cows on the common instead of two, he could add to his earnings. And four cows would bring him even more money from the sale of dairy products. Others added to their herds as well. Soon, however, the growing number of animals outstripped the limited size of the public pasture. In the town meeting, citizens heatedly argued out the problem of the common.

A boy growing up in those years could feel the local spirit of cooperation slowly giving way to the new pressures of competition. America of that time was moving rapidly toward the driving, aggressive mode of "free enterprise." To many this meant, "Get whatever you can for yourself, and let others do as best they can."

No wonder the pleasant common was disappearing in many towns! And along with it went the commonly owned forests and mills, and the New England custom of cooperating in home building and harvesting.

Something was happening to these gracious villages. George Marsh could see it in the view from Mount Tom, changing from year to year. The ax and the torch were leaving the hillsides bald. Cluttered with docks and milldams, the river was flooding its narrowing banks more frequently. The stony soil of the region was being farmed to the limit. Some of the changes in the vista below were clearly the work of nature. But in other changes, including some of the most destructive, George saw the hand of man.

Young Marsh heard about a grain-mill owner to the north who had taken it upon himself to tap a new source of water power. The miller enlisted the citizens of the town to help him dig a canal all the way to a nearby lake. Suddenly a flood was unloosed that swept through the valley, drowning cropland and forest and village, including the miller and his mill.

This was a story George Marsh never forgot. Into his eager mind he crowded a vast store of knowledge about the interplay of man and nature. Much of what he learned came from his own experiences while roaming the countryside alone.

Out of the boy's loneliness came a love of nature that was to deepen all of his life. Back across the years, he would recall that "the bubbling brook, the trees, the flowers, the wild animals, were to me persons, not things."

A man of parts

On his twenty-fifth birthday, George Perkins Marsh nailed up a shingle announcing that he was *Attorney at Law*. But if anyone was entitled to nail up ten other shingles as well, that man was Marsh.

His worrisome eye ailment sent him from one doctor to the next—without much help. But for a man who had to curb his reading, Marsh was already one of the most learned scholars in his state.

At a time when most youngsters were slowly tracing out their ABCs, George already had a good grasp of Greek and Latin, and he taught both subjects when he finished college. He took up new languages two at a time, learning French and Spanish and then later in quick succession German and Danish, Swedish and Icelandic. In time he mastered twenty languages, reading widely in all of them.

He seemed to forget nothing he had ever seen or read. And while still a very young man he was considered quite expert in fine art, mechanics, and natural science, and a well-qualified amateur in history and music.

George was now living in Burlington, Vermont, the state's largest city. He was well-settled and happily married, with two small sons. The law business did not excite him, and his office was mainly a base for dozens of other ventures. He was never a great financial success at any of them. Throughout his lifetime he was to seesaw back and forth between comfortable earnings and poverty and debt.

On an August afternoon in 1833, George hurried home to his wife, who had been ill. During the night she suddenly grew worse and died. That week Marsh's four-year-old son, Charles, was stricken with scarlet fever, and within eleven days he too was dead.

There were few friends to whom George could turn. To many people he seemed haughty, aloof. But he was a shy and gentle man, vulnerable to hurts. And he had built a wall between himself and the shocks of daily existence.

Marsh was like a person in a trance, overwhelmed by the double tragedy. Grief drove him to the edge of madness. But he fought for his sanity with work, taking on a series of demanding projects which allowed him not a moment of idleness. In the next years he raised purebred sheep, constructed roads and bridges, owned a woolen mill, edited a newspaper, sold lumber, operated a marble quarry, and ventured into politics.

If butcher, baker, and candlestick maker play differing roles in a community, Marsh wanted a share in them all. It was as though he sought the widest range of living experiences that men can have in a particular environment.

New worlds and old

Burlington took pride in its enterprising young citizen. This was a scenic, well-watered town facing the bright expanse of Lake Champlain. Like most New England towns, Burlington yearned for progress. The town newspaper was impatient for the day when "the loom, the shuttle, and the mechanical arts" would make full use of the town's "wasted" water power. Marsh's announcement that he would build a seven-story woolen mill brought a joyous response.

However, the mill, when completed, suffered a series of blows from nature and the international woolen market. Flood, fire, and ice crippled Marsh's operations. The steep fall of wool prices dealt the business a deathblow.

Marsh's fellow citizens in 1843 elected him to Congress. In Washington the Vermonter found time for a variety of projects

THE HAND OF MAN 45

and interests. He became interested in the founding of a new museum and library, the Smithsonian Institution. Marsh worked to make it a great showcase, exhibiting every possible view of the everyday life of the people in the setting of America's natural environment.

In the year 1847 Marsh came home to visit the places where he grew up. Startled and dismayed, he found everything changed for the worse, the quality of the living environment degraded. Smoky factories cast a pall over the towns. Sheep grazing, fire, and logging had ripped the green cover off the hillsides, now gullied and hideous. Nowhere in America had the soil been exhausted faster than in Vermont.

"Every middle-aged man who revisits his birthplace after a few years of absence," Marsh sadly told a gathering of farmers, "looks upon another landscape than that which formed the theater of his useful toils and pleasures."

On a May morning in 1849, Marsh received the startling news that he was appointed ambassador—to Turkey! There were many ways a man could view an assignment to a remote and troubled area. But Marsh looked forward eagerly to a chance to study that portion of the world where some of the earliest civilizations had begun.

Here man had carried on an age-old war with nature. What was the outcome of this struggle? What secrets were locked in the landscape of the Old World—and what could they mean for America?

Marsh was to uncover his own painful answers to such questions. The next fifteen years found him on three continents, making a deep and detailed study of man's effect on the environment. He handled his diplomatic duties in Turkey with skill and tact. And later President Abraham Lincoln made him United States Ambassador to Italy. Wherever Marsh traveled he pursued the study of the ancient ages, which had begun to absorb his life.

A small book that came into his hands during this period of his life shed light on a much older past. In *Origin of Species*, Charles Darwin revealed how life evolved on earth from its earliest simple forms to a vast array of species, man among them. To a world raised on the old Bible stories, Darwin's theories came as a thundering shock. The British biologist overturned the old ideas about life on earth.

Origin of Species opened up countless new paths for scientific exploration. And to Marsh the book was like a flash of lightning, illuminating dark corners of his own troubled thoughts. Darwin showed him more clearly than ever how living things were linked together, dependent on each other. Whenever new species appeared, they were adapted to the special conditions of life in which they found themselves. Marsh was also struck by Darwin's further conclusion—that species vanished when they were no longer able to adapt to their changing environments.

Links of life

Between journeys abroad, Marsh came home to Vermont, where he served his state in varied ways. One of his odd jobs was fish commissioner. And here he was confronted with a puzzling problem.

Vermonters jawed about it across their stone fences, asked hard questions in the town meetings, and wrote cranky letters to the local newspapers. On market days the same query could be heard from every mouth. "What has happened to the fish?"

Once the streams had been alive with trout, shad, and salmon. But year by year, the fish were fewer. Too often the angler went home with an empty creel and a riddle in his brain.

Marsh already had some clues. But he went at the problem with his usual thoroughness, like a detective solving a mystery. His answer pointed an accusing finger directly at his fellow citizens. "Yes, the fish are gone," he charged, "because you have seriously disturbed their life patterns."

As Vermonters gasped in amazement, the fish commissioner listed his charges. The local folk had polluted the rivers. They had shifted the drainage patterns by building dams and water-powered factories, by destroying foliage which once stored the rain water. Fishing heavily during the spawning season, they had interrupted the fishes' reproductive cycles. They had also reduced the insects and plants on which the small fry feed. Moreover, they had introduced into the state's waters the European pickerel, a voracious killer of the young of native fishes.

"All nature," Marsh added, "is linked together by invisible bonds. Every organic creature, however low, however feeble, however dependent, is necessary to the well-being of some other among the myriad forms of life with which the Creator has peopled the earth."

When Marsh returned to foreign duty as ambassador, he traveled widely. And wherever his duties took him, he became a student of the environment.

He had a deep appreciation of Old World cultures. Marsh was struck with admiration for the ageless record spread before him of man's painstaking efforts to cope with his surroundings. But he wondered too at the abundant evidences of failure.

He visited places where ancient writings described flourishing civilizations, rich in produce and commerce. Marsh found these sites as still as death, amid the rubble of deserted cities, silted harbors, boundless wasteland. He saw the evidence of forests destroyed, of soil turned barren, of bodies of water vanished, leaving salt and sand flats.

He felt a growing sense of alarm. Could it be true that all this waste and ruin was man's doing? His mind spanned thousands of years of history. Was it possible that the very civilizations that gave us so much science and philosophy, art and craftsmanship, had failed so utterly in their dealings with nature? The truth rushed at him from the barrenness of the surrounding hills and echoed across the man-made deserts.

Everywhere man had left his mark. But all too often it was a scene of discouragement and defeat. The wandering envoy found towns abandoned as inhabitants escaped the effects of their own pollution. Great deserts were formed when herds of domestic animals, grazing year-round, gleaned away the last shreds of grass. Cities were unwisely built in the flood plains. Flood and famine came as a direct result of man's abuse of the land, followed by ravaging epidemics.

Marsh put together a picture of nations trying to force the soil to produce too much, taxing the earth's resources, living richly for the moment with no thought for the future.

The ambassador brooded deeply about his findings. He was seized with fear, realizing the perils which modern civilizations now faced in their heedless quest for progress. Somehow the lessons of the past would have to be learned. Someone would have to sound a warning!

Slowly Marsh began work on a book. The subject was vast. But in time the facts began to arrange themselves into orderly patterns. The Vermonter wrote in a secluded Italian castle, his study heaped high with notes, data, references in dozens of languages. Here he put together the varied experiences and the gathered ideas of his lifetime.

Marsh's book began to take shape. Facts piled on facts. Each idea was carefully documented, footnoted. Out of months, years of tireless work came a thick manuscript, sober and scholarly. In its pages could be heard a cry of alarm.

Man and nature

"The earth is fast becoming an unfit home for its noblest inhabitant."

With these grim words, George Perkins Marsh summed up his book, *Man and Nature*. The large volume, which was published in 1864, covered a wide range of ideas, most of them never before touched upon by any writer. Certainly no one before had ever piled up such a powerful record of how man changes his living environment.

The squat, bearded, nearsighted man, now in his sixties, had told a disturbing story. But Marsh did not see man's works as being all bad. Nor did he urge him to abandon his present way of life and return to a simple, animal-like existence.

The Vermonter saw no sense in pining for the past. Aimed at an ever higher civilization, mankind's course was clear. Science, skills, and tools—these were now resources in moving toward a better life. There was no possible way for man to give up all that. However, Marsh seemed to be saying that man could use his good sense in dealing more wisely with the environment on which he depended for life.

Instead of wreaking a blind, relentless assault on nature, man could make a more careful use of soil and water and greenery. He could plan with foresight for his future needs. And he must become aware, said Marsh, of "the duties which this age owes to the next."

Marsh put a lot of faith in science to point the best way ahead. He urged a series of practical steps—for saving the forests, learning more about the proper use of the soils, controlling floods, irrigating the arid lands.

But he made it clear that through heedless action, "the ravages committed by man destroy the balance which nature has established." He added, "She avenges herself upon the intruder by letting loose her destructive energies." The human race, Marsh soberly warned, could become extinct.

A cry unheard

"Danger!" was Marsh's warning to his countrymen. "Men of the Old World have abused the land, with terrifying results. Are we now going to repeat all their tragic mistakes in America?"

Marsh's book did not become a best seller. Even the scientists of his time paid little attention to what he was trying to say. To them, his training seemed inadequate and his research too widely spread to be of much value. Instead of limiting his world to the laboratory, Marsh made his laboratory the entire world. But scientists studying life were becoming highly specialized. They had long since become accustomed to peering through lenses to get a closer and closer look at living matter. On the other hand, Marsh moved backward to achieve a wider view. His aim was to see life in broad perspective, to try to trace the large patterns of nature.

It was only a year or two after *Man and Nature* appeared that a new word was added to the language. "Ecology"—the term came to signify a special way of looking at the world. It was Marsh's way—a view that saw living things in motion against the backdrop of their environment, examining life as a complex web of changing relationships. Ecology was to become the science which studies living communities, where countless species interact with each other and with their physical surroundings. This was the study to which men would turn in time—to learn how they had unwittingly ruined their earthly home.

Years ahead of his time, Marsh used the methods of ecology to view problems of environment. He was an eyewitness to the spoilage of the the landscape. Unlike many with better eyesight, Marsh looked deeply into the inner causes of disturbing events.

From his embassy in the Italian Alps, Marsh had sounded an urgent alarm. Did America hear it? or heed it? In the late spring of 1864, when *Man and Nature* appeared, this country was in the grip of the Civil War. The bitter struggle was reaching a climax in the hills around the nation's capital.

Nor was his homeland ready to turn to Marsh's advice after the Civil War ended. Once the guns fell silent, a boom period began. Smoking factories poured out volumes of goods. A vast cropland was being farmed with new machinery. Gushers of "black gold" spouted from the earth. The West was opened to lumbering, mining, stock raising. Rivers were being bridged and dammed. Canals linked the waterways. The last miles of steel rail spanning the continent were being set into place.

America was now in a bold, expansive phase, boasting progress and abundance. From scientists and learned men the country demanded new inventions, better production methods, more effective ways of milking the resources of the nation. And its leaders were in no mood to listen to words of caution or restraint.

For many years Marsh's book was a lone outcry, sounding a shrill signal of distress. But above the din of commerce, the clangor of factories, the tumult of the cities, the sounds of "progress" —America seemed to hear nothing.

Frederick Olmsted

Wall Street 1848

Central Park 1858

The Country in the City

Central Park 1862

4. The Country in the City

*Hell is a city much like London—
A populous and a smoky city.*
          Percy Bysshe Shelley

New York City, 1840. The town throbbed with wild traffic running at a dizzy pace.

At dusk an army of office workers from the wholesale district poured into the busy streets. Bookkeepers and salesmen, railroad and shipping agents hurried toward cheap hotels, walk-up flats, boarding-house bedrooms.

A young man, just eighteen, marched in this joyless parade. He was Frederick Law Olmsted, a clerk for a dry-goods importer.

Like the many other newcomers to New York, Frederick was caught up in a bewildering pattern of city life. This was a world of noise, speed, and stress. The comforts seemed few. And yet the city was drawing new thousands daily.

Swept up in the headlong tide, young Olmsted moved down Broadway. His keen senses took it all in. Jumbled together in a single block were rooming houses and warehouses, cigar factories and brownstone homes, bars and butcher shops, stables and theaters.

Horses in harness clattered on the cobbles, singly or teamed in pairs, fours, or sixes. Vehicles ran in amazing variety—drays and hansom cabs, rubbish carts and omnibuses.

Crossing the street was sheer peril. You took a deep breath—and ran for your life! Suddenly a deafening whistle screamed. Swirling the dust, a fire company came racing by. Yesterday three children were burned to death in a Bowery firetrap. Tomorrow's *Sun* would tell how ten died in a burning garment factory.

To Frederick, New York was both fascinating and hideous. It was a city changing daily, building furiously. On its narrow carpet of land Manhattan spread northward and outward toward its fringe of wharves, squeezing itself skyward at last. Growing too fast, the city seemed to live for the day—planning nothing, ignoring tomorrow in order to answer today's shrill demands.

It was a town of buy and sell. A handful of persons lived richly in ornate mansions. The teeming thousands worked long drudging hours for a bare living.

The sounds of New York were high-pitched, raucous, jarring. In his dingy room the city crowded in on young Olmsted. The boy covered his ears, but still the frightening roar came through. In the streets below, the churning, frenzied, writhing stream of life flowed on all day and into the gaslit night.

A stranger in town

On Sunday Frederick was free for the day from filing invoices and stamping bills of lading. He unwound his mind from the endless yards of gingham and lace. Wanderer and watcher, he moved out across the strange urban world.

Frederick spent hours along a waterfront hemmed in with full-rigged vessels, hull to hull. This was America's busiest shipping center, linked by sail with a thousand distant ports. Frederick could hardly control his eagerness to travel. He knew that a wide world was waiting for him, and someday . . .

The young man enjoyed touring the theater district, the bustling hotels and restaurants, the brightly lit shops with goods from all the world arrayed in their show windows. Olmsted was a sensitive observer of his surroundings. His eye was a camera and his mind a filing cabinet. The vivid impressions that tumbled in on him left him with a jumble of strong feelings.

Thousands of foreign-born residents lived in the lower end of Manhattan. Frederick found these districts colorful. The clothing, customs, and languages reflected a rich mixture of people, and the air was filled with the smells of strongly flavored foods. But he was also deeply disturbed over the living conditions in these sections.

Homes long ago vacated by the well-to-do were split up from cellar to garret into many cubicles, each rented to an entire family. In these dark, airless firetraps the immigrant poor were huddled. Hardly any better were the new tenements being thrown up with the greatest speed and least cost possible. Into these huge boxlike structures people were packed as tightly as possible, with little regard for safety or health. The rents were far more than the tenants could afford.

These neighborhoods seemed to be gasping for breath. The only relief in the sultry summer heat was tiny Battery Park, jammed with Sunday crowds.

To Frederick the city's filth seemed almost unbearable. Numerous pigs, the city's scavengers, were turned loose to root in the dumps and gutters on their own. With dismay young Olmsted saw garbage and sewage being brought in carts and dumped into the East River.

The town's water supply was becoming dangerous and undrinkable. Some people collected rain water in barrels as it dripped from the roofs. "Country water" was peddled from wagons. On Bleecker Street, a householder tried to dig a well through four hundred feet of solid rock.

Was a city surrounded by water doomed to die of thirst? Or

would it succumb first to the numerous outbreaks of typhoid fever and other diseases which ravaged the crowded districts?

Frederick saw life in the city as a constant struggle for survival. He was sure he would never get used to living in New York. He felt like an outsider, an alien from another way of life.

Scenes of country life

His roots were in a rural America. During the years when Frederick was growing up, this was a nation that lived largely by a farmer's almanac. The four seasons were for sowing and growing, harvesting and storing. Events of the country year were the foaling of horses and the tasseling of corn, the southward flight of wildfowl and the river's icing over.

Frederick's memories of rural life were warm and glowing. Son of a prosperous New England merchant, he had lived as a free soul, close to nature, unbound by chores and routine.

Fred's mother died when he was still a small child. In an effort to give him a proper upbringing, the elder Olmsted arranged for his son's schooling in the homes of a series of country parsons. In these dour households Frederick acquired a distaste for both schooling and religion.

However, the boy was forever wandering off into the Connecticut countryside. He was welcomed by relatives in no fewer than ten farmsteads, where he often stayed overnight. There was a warm, open neighborliness among these people which he never found in the big city.

He still remembered the delights of his boyhood—the smells of charcoal making and potatoes roasting in the embers; the taste of maple syrup freshly boiled; the sound of apples crunching in the cider mill. He recalled flax growing in the field, being spun into yarn, and then being woven into linen cloth. At various times of the year the country household became absorbed in the making of soap, honey, or candles. There were Indian families in his neighborhood whom he watched at their crafts. He enjoyed setting up birdhouses for purple martins and listening to the talk around the stove at the village store.

What city boy, he now wondered, could match these glimmering memories of country life? What joys enriched a childhood on the steaming sidewalks of New York?

However, Frederick could see that year by year an increasing portion of America's people were becoming city dwellers. Thousands had already moved to the big centers of population. The young people on the farms were straining to get to the cities. But his own year of experience in New York had convinced him that there were serious shortcomings in urban life. And he wondered why people were so willing to exchange the peaceful habitat of the country for the harsh environment of the big town.

Could the city be made pleasant, comfortable, livable? The task appeared hopeless. For Frederick, the only course seemed to be escape. He planned to get out as soon as he could—while he still had his health and his sanity.

On the twenty-third of April, 1843, the bark *Ronaldson* prepared to sail from New York harbor, bound for China. Frederick Law Olmsted was one of the deck hands hauling up the anchor.

The young man's pulse quickened as the fluttering sails aloft caught the fullness of the wind. In a short time the worrisome city was far behind.

An unusual farmer

When the voyager came home at last, he took up farming in earnest. The farm he chose was located on Staten Island, just across the bay from New York City.

Frederick tackled every new enterprise with great zest, and he undertook farming with typical enthusiasm. He turned out to be an unusual farmer. During most of his life he had been making a deep study of growing things. On his Staten Island farm he produced a fine variety of wheat. And his turnips were the talk of the county.

The young farmer experimented with a wide range of shrubs and flowers, shade and fruit trees. He bought some newfangled machinery from England. From France he imported thousands of pear trees and planted an orchard. Around the old Dutch farmhouse Frederick showed his talent for landscape work. He turned the farm into a show place—although it didn't show much profit.

Frederick looked more like an artist than like a farmer. He was slight of build, and he was neat in appearance even when working out in the field. His dark hair, combed back from his high forehead, grew long and wavy. His wide-set eyes seemed to tell everything about him, his sensitive thoughtfulness and his inner store of strength and will.

From the window seat in his house, the young farmer had a magnificent view across the bay. The blue waters were flecked with whitecaps and white sails. At dusk the lighthouses could be seen winking from a dozen rocky points. In the distance, New York City arose from the ocean mist as if by magic. Its towers and spires were the beginnings of what would someday be a famous skyline.

The ferry from the city brought boatloads of friends. On weekends the Olmsted farm became a holiday place for a lively group of young men and women. The farmhouse resounded with entertainment and absorbing conversation about world affairs. The young farmer was fascinated. There were chores to be done— beans to be picked and a fence to be mended. But they could wait for another day.

At times the discussion became a storm, with Frederick in the eye of it. The talk often ran late on Saturday night and was renewed on Sunday. Most controversial of all was the topic of slavery and the growing crisis between North and South.

Frederick, full of curiosity about actual conditions in the South, planned a trip into the slave states. It was to be the first of a number of such fact-finding journeys into other parts of America and abroad.

Gradually Olmsted was losing interest in the farm. Many other things drew his attention. His mind was too keen to be fettered by dull routine. And his interests were too broad to be bound by the barnyard.

An urban environment

Travel led to writing, and Frederick's graphic accounts of his trips began to appear in the New York newspapers. During this time he also became involved in several publishing ventures. But his main effort went into the writing of several books.

These were more than just travel books. Each of them tried to examine how people live in various environments. They attempted to deal with the relationship of men to their surroundings. Frederick's deepest concern was with ordinary people, going through their everyday pursuits against the background of their own communities. He began to look in the same thoughtful manner at life in the high-towered city across the bay.

New York City was creating problems for itself as fast as it grew. However, it seemed that on the very brink of complete disaster, the anger of the people brought some solution to each new crisis. The city solved its water problem in dramatic fashion: pipes were run up into the Catskill Mountains to bring down a flow of pure water into Manhattan reservoirs.

But in many other ways the quality of the environment grew worse. New York reeled from one epidemic to the next. Cholera, tuberculosis, yellow fever—these took hundreds of victims daily.

It would be years before scientists were to develop the germ theory, making the clear connection between certain diseases and tiny unseen organisms. However, Frederick Olmsted was aware of some link between the ills of city people and the conditions under which they lived. Clearly, disease throve in the shadows of the tenements. The filthy streets were a breeding place for plague, the open sewers a source of typhoid. He was convinced that the city's health problems would never be solved without sun and open space and greenery.

Olmsted read the grim reports of an organization that had been formed "for the improvement of the condition of the poor." On Oliver Street investigators found "a miserable rear dwelling . . . which contains fourteen families." On Cherry Street they went through a tenement house of five airless, overcrowded stories containing more than five hundred persons. Some of the most sickening living quarters were in wet cellars. The most dangerous were the high firetraps from which there was no escape.

Nor was New York an unusual case. Across America the booming cities each had their critical problems. A vast stretch of barracks, newly built for St. Louis workers, turned rapidly into a gray slum. Coal smoke from the mills filled Pittsburgh's air with soot. Sewage oozed from the unpaved streets of New Orleans. Chicago doubled in size in ten years, a young giant growing out of its breeches—and unable to keep up with the mounting needs of its people.

The railroad and the telegraph, extending into the farthest back country, were changing America. Every bushel of wheat raised on a Kansas farm was traded in the Chicago grain exchange. The lives of cattlemen, fruit gardeners, and cotton growers were regulated by railroad and shipping firms located on Wall Street in New York. There was now a central market place for what America produced, and its location was in the city.

The big towns swarmed with new arrivals—a landless population needing store-bought food and clothing. The city streets were filled with fresh-faced boys and girls who came to work for cash wages and to stake their survival on a job. For newcomers from the countryside and from rural areas abroad, this was their first experience with the special problems of living in close daily contact with thousands. To many, the hazards of city life—disease, crime, poverty—came as a shock.

Frederick Olmsted saw commerce and industry advancing at a great rate. Huge private fortunes were being built. But life was hardly improving for the working men and women who made it all possible. The most "successful" merchants, employers, or landlords were those who paid the lowest wages, demanded the highest rents—and gave the least attention to the outcries of the people. As for the local politicians, their plea was that the poor conditions were "temporary" and would certainly improve—after the next election.

Central Park

In the late summer of 1856, Frederick spent some time at a seaside resort near New York. A book he had written, dealing with his travels in the back country of Oklahoma and Texas, needed some finishing touches.

He was now thirty-five years old, and neither farming nor book writing had turned out as he had hoped. Strolling along the seashore, he thought deeply about his life and the fact that somehow he had not yet found his special role. It was an age of the specialist—and Frederick Olmsted was a man with a broad range of interests. He was an acute observer of people, with a wide knowledge about the way men live in varied environments. Unfortunately, such learning did not point toward any particular profession or career. To some he appeared to be an idler, a failure, a misfit.

The day's wandering along the sunny beach filled him with a sense of disappointment. His life seemed as aimless as a gull's flight. The sand dollars reminded him of his mounting debts!

At teatime Olmsted turned back toward the inn. In the dining room he was drawn into a conversation about New York City's snarled efforts to build a large public park. The undeveloped land had been purchased, a vast area of more than one square mile on the northern rim of the city. However, the actual construction of a park was hopelessly bogged down in a nasty political wrangle. The money for the project was being held up in the city council. Workmen had been hired to clear the land—but they had begun working on the basis of promises instead of wages.

Olmsted's companion in the dining room was Charles Eliot Norton, one of the commissioners of the park. He explained that the Central Park project was not only without money, but also without a superintendent. Olmsted was keenly interested in the park and voiced his strong views about it. Suddenly the conversation took a strange turn. Looking squarely at Olmsted, the commissioner said to him: "Why don't you take the position as superintendent yourself?"

"*I* take it?" Olmsted responded, completely surprised. "I'm not sure I wouldn't, if it were offered to me."

"Well, it won't be offered," said Norton, "but if you'll go to work, I believe you may get it. I wish that you would!"

"You are serious?" asked Frederick, disbelieving.

Norton replied that there was no time to lose, and he suggested to Olmsted how he should go about applying for the job.

Some weeks went by while all the vying political factions investigated this unknown man who was seeking to become the superintendent of Central Park. What weighed most heavily in Olmsted's favor was the fact that his political record was a complete blank. Shortly afterward, Frederick Law Olmsted had the job.

"Lungs" of the city

A first trip through the park property would have discouraged some people. Olmsted was led through the most dismal wasteland he had ever seen. He waded knee-deep in foul-smelling muck. The grounds had been used for many years by squatters whose businesses made them outcasts from the town—operators of slaughterhouses, garbage dumps, pigsties, and other such slimy and reeking nuisances. To many people, the idea of making a park out of such a place seemed ridiculous. There was laughter too at the very idea of calling it *Central* Park. This was a vile sinkhole on the edge of town that you passed as rapidly as possible on your way toward the villages of Yorkville or Harlem.

The sheer chaos of the place challenged Frederick's sense of beauty and order. Moreover, the possibilities of this great project fired his imagination. What he needed now was the authority to carry out his own ideas.

A contest had been announced for the best complete plan for the new park, with a prize for the winner. Frederick found a partner, an architect named Calvert Vaux, and the two of them set to work on a design. Olmsted now plunged into the competition with driving eagerness. He and Vaux combed over every inch of the park site to study its terrain. They worked through the night at the drawing board, Frederick setting down the details in written form.

For Olmsted, the winning of the award came as the high point of his life. Suddenly it seemed that the years of drifting and uncertainty had had some purpose after all. Olmsted's work on the park design was the creation of a man who was not bound by a narrow training or experience. Everything he had learned in his wandering travels became a part of the plan. And all his groping to find the true meaning of the city went into the making of his design.

With the last obstacle out of the way, Frederick moved ahead rapidly on what was to be his masterpiece. He saw it as a work of art, with all the parts flowing harmoniously from a single unified pattern. No other city in America or anywhere else in the world had attempted anything on so vast a scale. No public park had

THE COUNTRY IN THE CITY   65

ever involved so much moving of earth, draining of swamps, planting, road building, or digging of artificial ponds.

Gradually a tangle of underbrush re-emerged as a flower garden. Boggy lowland was converted into playing fields. What was formerly a swamp became a lagoon for boating in summer and skating in winter. At the same time Olmsted made the most of the area as he found it. In some sections the park retained its rustic appearance, with rough outcroppings of rock and scenic wooded areas in their natural state.

In the back of Frederick's mind as he worked was the vivid picture of the common people of the city in the ugly and crowded places where they labored and lived. This was to be their park. Olmsted stated its purpose clearly. It was, he said, "to supply to the hundreds of thousands of tired workers, who have no opportunity to spend their summers in the country, a specimen of God's handiwork that shall be to them what a month or two in the mountains is to those in easier circumstances."

He hoped to bring a natural setting to the city. Somewhere in this huge open space the weary worker might find refreshment in the greenery, solitude from the overcrowded tenements, a healthful day of play and rest. He saw public parks as "the lungs" of the city, a source of strength and energy.

Every large town, Olmsted believed, owed at least this much to its citizens. "All wealth is a result of labor," he declared, "and without recuperation and recreation, the power of each individual to add to the wealth of the community is soon lost."

"Sunday in Central Park" became one of New York's finest attractions. With the first pleasant days of spring, families gathered for walks along the mall. The sparkling fountains attracted many. On Wednesday and Saturday evenings, band concerts were given in the pavilion. People went for scenic drives along the winding boulevards in carriages drawn by sleek grays and lanky trotters. Young couples were attracted to the rowboats, sharing the lagoon with graceful swans.

In the cold months, the park came alive with winter sports. Many waited for the word that "the ball is up!," the signal that the ice on the lake was safe. On a single Sunday evening, as many as twenty thousand people skated, swaying under the lights amid the snowy hills and shimmering trees.

The city beautiful

Frederick delighted in the park and its success. But there were dark days when he was ready to give it all up. He found himself and the park caught in the cross fire of opposing political factions. Olmsted fought hard to protect the park from corruption. However, the city government had come under the domination of the notorious political boss, William Marcy Tweed. Frederick was torn by demands from job seekers. Rival city officials vied for control of the park payroll. His work was hampered by interfering politicians who sought contracts for their friends.

In the years that followed, Olmsted resigned in anger several times from his position as head of Central Park. But again and again he returned to resume a work charged with meaning for him. Between these times, however, he carried out tasks that for other men might have been a life's work.

The outbreak of the Civil War found him in charge of a great humanitarian movement to aid the victims of the struggle. He was the head of the United States Sanitary Commission, which was later to become the American Red Cross.

With the war's end, Olmsted went west to help bring into being the first of America's national parks. A visit to California's magnificent Yosemite Valley stirred in Olmsted the hope that such sites might be protected from spoilage and made into recreation areas for the use of the people. He joined a movement that was to create not only Yosemite National Park but an extensive chain of such natural playgrounds across the United States.

For a time, Olmsted was an editor of *The Nation,* a magazine which he helped to found. He became involved in a crusade to clean up the unsightly mess at Niagara Falls, where the water's edge was cluttered with mills and power plants, the shacks of hucksters and souvenir peddlers, shoddy hotels and resorts.

Something new was happening across America. People were becoming conscious as never before of the beauty of this land, the glory of natural places and the healthfulness of outdoor recreation. A famous New England statesman, Daniel Webster, underscored the new spirit in amusing fashion. On a trip to the West, Webster refused to sit inside the stuffy railroad cars. Instead he mounted his rocking chair on an open flatcar so that he "might better enjoy the scenery," and rocked his way across the country.

Traveling vacations came into style. Americans began flocking each summer to seaside and mountain resorts, many venturing into wilderness areas to hike and camp. Outdoor sports, for both players and viewers, became popular. The game of baseball was already taking the cities by storm.

Frederick Olmsted's Central Park emerged as a model for the nation. Almost every city began in this period to build parks and playgrounds, sports fields and public gardens. The grimiest of the industrial towns began to look at themselves with a critical eye and make some changes. Some reclaimed a lake front that they had surrendered to the railroads, or a river front cluttered with warehouses. By his example, Olmsted became the leader of what was later known as the "city beautiful" movement. And his services were in demand everywhere.

His calling card now read: *Frederick Law Olmsted, Landscape Architect.* Many scratched their heads in wonder at the strange title. An architect, they thought, was a man who designed buildings. But Olmsted was less interested in buildings than in the spaces between them. He had in fact created a brand-new profession.

Frederick's work centered more and more in the growing cities. And his experience in these years slowly changed his deep fear and dislike of city life. He saw the fate of all America mirrored in its urban scene.

"Our country has entered upon a stage of progress in which its welfare is to depend on the convenience, safety, order, and economy of life in its great cities," he wrote. "America cannot gain in virtue, wisdom, comfort except as its cities also advance."

He could understand clearly now why the city had become such a powerful magnet. Here were opportunities and many choices. In contrast to farm or village, the city offered a wide range of careers, education, fellowship, entertainment. Olmsted saw immigrants attending night schools, young people caught up in the gaiety of the city's social life, farmers learning skilled trades, wide-eyed newcomers taking in lectures and ball games, museums and concerts, winter carnivals and summer picnics.

Because of their wealth, Frederick saw the possibilities for urban communities to become "humanizing centers of cultural and intellectual activity," as well as safe and convenient places in which to live. He now saw the city's promise as an environment planned for man. The key to it all, Olmsted believed, was in the city's over-all design. How was the community planned—and for whom? These were the vital questions.

Unfortunately, much of the American city was in the grip of its land dealers. They planned it to suit themselves. There was little room for beauty or charm. The ugly structures they built were intended solely to bring the greatest possible income. No footage was wasted on a tree or a patch of grass. In vain Olmsted pleaded that communities must be designed with "much larger open spaces, open to sunlight and fresh air."

All the American cities were losing out to planlessness. Every day workmen were building tomorrow's slums. And Frederick Law Olmsted could painfully see the future of the crowded tenement districts.

Planned suburb

In New York City one day, Olmsted met a young woman who had "run in to do a little shopping." She would be back home by suppertime on a farm miles away. He pieced this incident together with reports he heard frequently now of people working in the city who traveled daily to homes in the countryside. A thousand other clues pointed to closer links developing between the city and its surrounding area.

In the restless mind of Frederick Olmsted appeared a vision. His idea was to create a new type of environment. His own experiences had given him bits and pieces of a design for living: easy access to places of work; the rich cultural opportunities found in modern cities; spacious natural surroundings and scenic beauty; roomy dwellings built with comfort and privacy, and still within the financial reach of people with moderate means.

He had seen many suburbs around American cities and abroad. But none suited his idea of what was possible. In his mind there began to form the picture of a totally planned community. The opportunity to bring this picture to life came shortly. He was invited to design a completely new town on a riverbank six miles from Chicago.

In the 1870s, Olmsted's "Riverside" appeared out of the prairie land. It was a pleasant, tree-shaded village, trim and well-arranged. Its houses were set among quiet, winding lanes, no two of them alike, but all grouped in a well-balanced pattern. Railroad and carriage routes put the "urban villagers" within easy reach of the city.

Olmsted's model didn't turn out exactly as he had hoped. For one thing, its homes were priced too high. Riverside developed many of the shortcomings of the so-called "bedroom community," with people separated by time and distance from their work places. This suburb was unsuited to the automobile age, which was soon to make its explosive appearance.

But Olmsted had produced something bold and original that set a widening trend. This was not the kind of suburb which grew wild on the city's edge, but rather a carefully planned attempt at combining the best of both rural and urban features. Riverside was in fact a major advance in town planning, a joint undertaking of many private owners who agreed to become partners in an overall community design.

The planner envisioned the city of the future as a great wheel with scores of suburbs at its outer rim. But how easily the wheel could get stuck in the mire of political rivalry! Olmsted could see the jealousy and bitterness and conflict growing between the urban and suburban governments.

His answer was an administrative setup that would cover the city as well as its surrounding communities. And he proposed to give that agency the power to deal with the needs of the entire district.

Environmental problems, he argued, have no respect for man-made boundaries. Air and water pollution do not stop at the city limits. The planning of good transportation, sewage disposal, fire and police protection were common needs for all the area's residents. Such a unified governing agency, he hoped, would be able to plan attractive suburbs in those outlying areas not yet settled.

New York City in those years was limited to Manhattan. But this small island was already the hub of a large regional circle of closely connected communities. Olmsted urged the formation of a single administration to cover the entire metropolitan area. The planner was an old man with a gray beard before he saw the establishment of Greater New York, a consolidation of five boroughs, including numerous villages and suburbs.

In his declining years, Olmsted continued to fight for the lost values of natural beauty in the large centers of civilization. And he was a stubborn fighter, venting his wrath on politicians and private operators who stood in his way.

He returned always to the urban region and its problems. For here, he sensed, was the scene of America's fight for its future. Overwhelmingly, the people by free choice were fundamentally changing their environment from country to city. And the nation's real destiny lay in that new habitat.

For Olmsted, the master planner, there could no longer be any doubt about tomorrow's trend. This was to be an urban civilization. In his own lifetime he had seen the beginnings of this change.

In this same span of nineteenth-century years, another boy would grow up in a Wisconsin farmhouse where a homemade clock ticked rhythmically through the quiet night. John Muir was to awaken suddenly to a changing America.

John Muir

Thunder on the Mountain

5. Thunder on the Mountain

How blundering they were, these white people—whose very presence mysteriously denuded the land of the buffalo that were its wealth, and who befouled rivers that were the homes of great spirits. . . .
From the Ojibway legend of how
God created the white man

The stillness of the predawn hours was shattered by a loud crash. In the roused farmhouse there was a brief hush, and then a voice called up the stairs, "What on earth was that?"

"Only me," replied John, "gettin' up."

By some weird power, the bed had suddenly raised itself on end and dumped the sleeping boy to the floor. Someone had taught that bed to stir itself and perform strange tricks before either sunup or cockcrow. The magic bed was the handiwork of John Muir, junior inventor. He called it his "early-rising machine." And he had the bruises to prove how well it worked.

To Johnny's aching backside there would be added a few more sore spots. In the Muir household, a severe thrashing was the sure penalty for any such droll behavior. There was no nonsense tolerated under the roof of Daniel Muir. He was a stern father whose strict beliefs came word for word from the Bible.

"The very devil's in that boy," he muttered to himself as he applied a stout switch. Daniel saw no cruelty in his punishments.

He was simply beating the devil out of his son—a service to God, and to the boy as well.

Young John gave in sullenly to the whipping. But in his mind he was already a rebel. The auburn-haired lad was growing himself a stringy red beard. He was sixteen and strongly built, six feet tall in his homespun socks. In some ways he felt himself to be a prisoner in that mid-Wisconsin farmstead. But he sensed also the deep stirring of power within him that would one day break him loose from all bondage.

Stolen moments

The Muirs had come from Scotland in 1849 when John was eleven years old. It was a rock-strewn and rolling countryside in which they settled, amid gurgling streams and groves of shady oaks. With two brothers and four sisters, John was raised in the simple routine of the frontier farm.

The Muir house was a cold, austere shell. No pictures adorned the walls, and no bit of carpet graced the bare floor. The sound of laughter was never heard at Daniel Muir's dinner table. Time was not to be "wasted" on play or poetry, frills or fancies. Idleness was a sin and gaiety the height of wickedness.

But the Muir children were full of cheerfulness, and no strict rules could curb their inner merriment. Skillfully they avoided the purple anger and the punishing rod of Daniel Muir. They danced a wild jig behind his back and broke into gay song and laughter when he was well out of hearing. Most of all they rejoiced secretly in the beauty of the natural surroundings.

The early spring was Johnny's own special time. He listened for the wild, sad cry of the loon and the cracking of ice in the lake. In the chill March days he searched for the cheering blossoms of the windflower, first to appear above the frozen ground.

With his brother, John played doctor to an injured bird. They lay at the lake's edge admiring the water bugs. And they learned to swim by copying the kick of the frog. The spring came to a glorious end with a feast of wild strawberries. The boys ran carefree across the sandy hills, feeling oneness with the earth and wonder at its beauty.

But such precious moments were few. When he was still small enough to walk under the plow handles, John was already toiling with a team of oxen, cutting the furrows straight enough to suit his father. The chores were heavy and endless. John, the eldest son, split rails for the zigzag fences. He carried water and feed to the animals, ground the scythes, hoed the corn, chopped the firewood. There was no moment for rest—or even for illness. Every hour from rising to bedtime was filled with work, meals, or family worship.

Daniel Muir believed in an angry, punishing God—and he volunteered his assistance. He saw his main mission as keeping his family on the narrow path of holiness. God was served through work—and the harder the toil, the more holy.

Hear the Word!

In driving his family mercilessly, the elder Muir was hardly considered uncommon among the family men of his time and place. The countryside was full of such men.

They flocked into the village churches to be reminded of their sinfulness. Repeatedly they heard the words of Genesis which seemed to spell out their duties. "Replenish the earth, and subdue it," they were told. "Have dominion over the fish of the sea, and over the fowl of the air, and over every living thing that moveth upon the earth."

On Sunday the God-fearing farmer was told that he was not a part of nature, but its master. He was the center of a universe made to serve his needs. And early on Monday morning he resumed his vigorous battle against nature, strengthened by the belief that all of it was his to conquer.

He followed a path made by the tiller of the soil in past ages. Always he had held the power of life and death over his small segment of the earth. He chose among species of plants and animals. On the North American continent he decided that the grazing animals should be cattle and sheep instead of buffalo and deer. He substituted cornstalks for grass, cut away a maple grove to make room for a pigsty. Often he replaced a hundred wild species with a single protected one. Countless living things were outlawed as pests, weeds, or varmints. He divided all of nature into the "useful" and the "worthless."

In making the land serve his needs, the farmer seldom reckoned the effect on the natural environment. Rarely did he pause to consider that there might be alternative ways to achieve his food-producing goals. If there was anything in his Bible that warned him to deal cautiously with the land, the pious farmer never found it.

Instead he moved relentlessly without ever realizing that he was upsetting ageless natural patterns, without ever reflecting as to what the consequences might be. Often he sucked out of the soil its last bit of fertility. He killed off the small animals that would have kept the crop-devouring insects in check. And he stripped the moisture-hoarding trees from hillsides—without understanding that he was thereby lowering the level of the underground water.

Hard rock

With the springs gone dry on the Muir farm, his father one day ordered John to begin a brutally hard task, the digging of a well. The boy shoveled through ten feet of gravel—and reached bedrock. From then on, John was lowered by means of a bucket and rope, armed with a hammer and a mason's chisel.

Day by day the boy inched his way deeper, pounding out bits of hard rock. The weary weeks found him cramped into the bottom of a slender shaft from early morning until long after dark. And still there was no sign of water.

One morning young John was lowered eighty feet to the bottom of the bore. Suddenly he felt faint. The narrow walls began to spin. He was being choked by poisonous gas seeping from the rock. Gasping for breath, he struggled to call for help.

His father, hearing no sound out of the dark pit, shouted, "What's wrong down there?"

Silence. And then a distant, feeble murmur, "Take me out." The bucket was hauled up rapidly with the boy slumped over it.

Luckily, he was still alive—but barely so. The deadly chokedamp had filled his lungs almost to suffocation. John was carried to the house, where the anxious family gathered around him. Gradually he was breathing normally again, relieved at his narrow escape. The boy was permitted a day or two of rest. But soon he was in the bottom of the shaft again. He chipped doggedly at the rock—until he struck water at last.

If water was a growing problem, the land became an even greater one. Each new crop was smaller than the last. The thin, sandy soil was giving out. Daniel Muir struck back by farming more intensively, seeding winter wheat as soon as the autumn harvest was over. The farm was going downhill, but Daniel Muir continued to punish the earth. He countered by putting the plow to new sections of land.

The Wisconsin countryside was filling up. Immigrants came like wind-borne seeds, striking earth and taking root. Young John Muir could see the frontier moving westward. Waves of homeseekers were settling the Middle West, but the bolder pioneers were moving on. The boy grew increasingly restless, knowing that his roving time would come.

One day the Muir children gaped wide-eyed as a winged tide swept across the sky—passenger pigeons! There were multitudes of the long-tailed, graceful birds. "Oh, what colors!" the children gasped. "Look at those breasts, as bonnie as roses."

The huge flocks came in waves, settling in the trees and under them to feed on acorns. During each migration their coming was awaited by armed men. Large numbers fell with each firing of a shotgun. The elegant birds were easy prey for hunters, who carried them off by the armload.

The Muir children cried out in dismay to see the birds shot down. But once again it was the pious elders of the community who sanctioned the killing of these beautiful creatures. "Aye, it is a pity," they said, "but they were made to be killed and sent for us to eat."

John Muir wouldn't have dreamed then that the lifetime on earth of the passenger pigeon would be no longer than his own. Within half a century, a lone passenger pigeon would die in a Cincinnati zoo, the last of its species.

Tinker with time

In stolen moments on the farm, John read a few snatches from a borrowed book of poems. Or he carved secretly at bits of hickory wood which he always carried in his pockets.

He fashioned gears and levers. In some strange way, the intricate workings of a clock pieced themselves together in his untrained mind. And out of his whittling came a crude but practical time piece, ticking with an odd wooden sound and loudly striking the hours.

His tools were simple and homemade. And yet there seemed to be no end to what he could construct. To Daniel Muir, his son's inventions were just so much "nonsense." But John built a machine for feeding the horses at any desired hour. Another contrivance would light fires automatically. He experimented with water wheels and windmills to provide sources of power for farm work.

These were devices that came out of John's torment, his rebellion against a life of endless toil. He was trapped in the struggle for time of his own. And in looking for some escape, he turned to inventions that were laborsaving and timesaving.

Neighbors were dumfounded at the boy's originality. What they saw was a remarkable home-grown talent. There was no telling what Johnny Muir might accomplish with education and training. They encouraged the lad to continue his tinkering and to seek help in carrying out his ideas.

But John had been brought up to have a poor opinion of himself. He had been told a thousand times that he was of no account, a worthless sinner, lower than the earthworm. And he found it hard to believe anything else.

It took some urging by his friends—but somehow, John Muir was aboard a train on a late September morning in the year 1860. He was on his way to the state fair at Madison—with his inventions strapped to his back.

Each for all

The fair was a bedlam of squealing pigs and shouting medicine peddlers, roaring threshers and carnival hubbub. But nothing rivaled the goggle-eyed wonder of Johnny Muir and his handmade contraptions. Farm folk, state officials, students from the nearby university crowded around the bearded young inventor. The praise made young John lightheaded. He explained until he was hoarse. And in a mood of pride and daring, he took the second bold step of his life.

The farm boy, with his backwoods schooling, climbed the steps of the state university. He could hardly believe it when he was told yes—he would be admitted! However, it would be hard work to manage his studies as well as earning his livelihood. Hard work? John knew all about that. In fact, he had never known any other way to live.

In the next four years, John Muir eagerly made up for all the reading and learning that he had missed. He was like a starved man turned loose in a bakeshop. Greedily he helped himself to whatever tasted good—botany, Greek, poetry, geology.

He was warned that his haphazard course of study would not lead to a degree, a profession, a career. But he laughed, unconcerned. His life's work would be to find meanings in nature. And he had already learned that the natural world would not fit into tiny compartments.

"Everything is hitched to everything else," he liked to say. "Each for all and all for each."

There was wondrous order in this universe—full of great clockwork rhythms and intricate patterns of constant change. Young John delighted in his fresh discoveries. And everywhere he saw the astonishing beauty of it all—blossom color and bird song, millions of glowworms throbbing with light, and the sublime grandeur of a summer storm.

His school years were over all too quickly. John Muir was coming to another of his life's big choices. It was 1865. The long agony of the Civil War was ending, and now the nation was moving wearily toward a welcome peace. President Lincoln's Homestead Act had opened government land to individual claims. The postwar trend was toward recovery, stability, settlement.

All about him John Muir heard advice about what he should do with his 25-year-old life. "Take a job." "Settle down." "Buy a farm." "Find your place."

One spring morning he packed a few needs in a little bag and took off. His steady, loping gait carried him northward, toward Canada's pine trees and cold lakes. Light-footed and lighthearted, he strode across the open countryside. John traveled at random and camped in simple fashion. With neither gun nor fishhook he made scarcely a sound or a ripple in the wilderness. Needing little in order to sustain himself, he set a life-style of asking as little as possible from his environment. He saw himself "free as a bird, independent alike of roads and people." The long months of wandering left him penniless but feeling gloriously enriched by his intimate contacts with nature.

The cold northern days now ended early. Like some burrowing animal, John looked for a winter home. He found a place to live, and a job in a factory which made handles for rakes and brooms. A friendly group of Scots ran the plant and John was made welcome. They soon learned to their surprise that the wayfaring lad they had hired was a master at woodworking. Moreover, he was ingenious with machines.

John's tinkering with a lathe doubled the factory's output of broom handles. His feat drew much praise and John reveled in his own skill. But as he sauntered in the nearby woods at dusk, he was filled with uneasiness.

The towering trees around him deepened his sense of guilt. How long would he go on seeing these great tree boles turned into saw logs, the logs into boards, and the boards into rake handles? He had already been asked to become a partner in the plant—or was it really a partnership in the destruction of the forests?

He sensed too that his inventions no longer served any great need in his life. They would never satisfy his deeper hunger.

Much as he was drawn toward mechanical things, he had a vague feeling that they reached out to capture him. Was he now to be tied to a machine, as he had once been bound to the land?

John slept in a little cabin near the plant. A howling blizzard roared in the chimney on the night of March 1. Tossing in his sleep, John suddenly came wide-awake. The window framed a raging fire! Gale-driven flames quickly destroyed the woodworking factory, and by morning there were only embers.

Moving on now, John headed southward. The fire seemed to settle matters for him—but not quite. The turmoil still raged within him. "I should like to invent useful machinery," one side of him urged. And then came the reply. "You do not wish to spend your life among machines."

"Earth Planet, Universe"

The late spring found him in Indianapolis, Indiana. Once again he was employed at woodworking, making wagon parts in a big steam-driven factory. Here too his mechanical talents were put to good use.

In the darkened workshop John stayed alone one night to repair a drive belt. In order to loosen the belt, he pried hard against it with a chisel. Suddenly the sharp tool turned and sprang, striking his eyes. John felt his eye-fluid wet in his hand. Crying out in pain and terror, he was plunged into utter darkness.

Blind! The horror of it gripped him. Flashing through his mind ran the pictures of what he would never see again. In that moment he knew what was dear to him in life. How could he live without his eyes, he sobbed, "closed forever on all God's beauty?"

In the next weeks, under a doctor's care, John lay despairing in a dark room. By touch he scrawled letters to friends. "I am lost," he wrote, "lost in the darkness of a terrible valley." But gradually out of the depths of gloom came insight and new hope. No matter how this nightmare would end, the way ahead for him was clear. He could never put himself in bondage to either men or machines. Sustaining himself somehow, he would live the life of a free man.

Then came the joyous news that he was not to be blind. After some weeks of rest his sight would be fully restored. Each day that followed brought a new revelation of light and wonder. He was like a man released from a dungeon. A hundred wild calls now sounded in his ears and the promise of nature's marvels beckoned from the horizon.

He was soon foot-loose again, off on a thousand-mile walk south to the Gulf, and then on to the West. In a small rubber bag he carried a clamping device for pressing plants, a sketchbook, and a journal for recording his thoughts. On the flyleaf of the blank book he inscribed his name and address: *John Muir, Earth Planet, Universe.*

It was April now, and just ahead were the first high mountains he had ever seen in his life. He was content and scot-free, choosing what he called the "wildest, leafiest, least-trodden way."

John shuddered when he thought about what he left behind and how narrowly he escaped. He had been in great danger, he said to himself, the danger of becoming so successful at his job that he might have destroyed the true meaning of his life.

He paused on a quiet hillside that evening to write in his journal: "I might have become a millionaire, but I chose to become a tramp!"

The high Sierra

The stranger looked completely lost on busy Market Street, San Francisco. At last he stopped a passer-by, asking, "Can you tell me the quickest way out of town?"

On that foggy March morning the wanderer felt himself being

studied with some curiosity—his rustic clothes, wind-swept beard, sun-darkened cheeks.

"Just where do you want to go?"

"Any place where it's wild," replied John Muir.

The wilderness he found was in the Sierra Nevada, the awesome saw-tooth range rising skyward from the central valley of California. "The range of light," he called it. From the moment he arrived, he was completely at home. This was a region wild and wide, with enough towering grandeur in its peaks and forests to lift his spirits to soaring heights. Here he had enough room to roam for a lifetime.

The West, when John Muir came to it in 1868, was a sparsely settled frontier. To most Americans it was the symbol of adventure—and abundance. Orators declaimed their praise of "the Golden West" with its "endless forests," "boundless plains," and "topless heights," its rivers "teeming with salmon" and its wild game in limitless quantities.

And yet, in the midst of all this lavish plenty, there were some disturbing signs of scarcity. Beyond Omaha and Kansas City the lands were arid. The rains came seldom and water was in short supply. Bitter struggles were raging over water rights. The range lands were being turned into a battleground as larger and larger livestock herds devastated the grasses and turned green areas into deserts. Gradually some of the forests were disappearing.

Before the Civil War began, the grazing land of buffalo was cut in two by the Union Pacific Railroad. And by the end of the 1870s the southern herd was wiped out.

In these years written accounts of life in the West were popular features in the newspapers and magazines. And over the signature of John Muir, Americans began to read of a West as wondrous as it was wild. Daily, Muir jotted into his journal his keen, close, detailed observations about a natural world remote from civilization, and in time this rich lore found its way into print.

For months at a time he lived alone on desolate heights among eagles and glaciers and age-old trees twisted by the roaring winds. He explored hidden gorges, spectacular cascades, and vast ice fields where no one had ever set foot before. Occasionally he came out of the wilderness to replenish his supplies of bread and tea.

John, lean and lithe, had a cat's grace. He climbed sheer canyon walls with a sureness of hand and foot. Exulting in nature's raw power, he responded joyously to a storm or an earthquake. And he danced in ecstasy across flower-strewn meadows.

Most men think of wilderness in terms of hardship and danger. But Muir felt completely secure in the natural setting. Fearless, he lived unarmed among bears, snakes, and mountain lions—and no harm ever came to him.

Part of the time he was shepherd, carpenter, or mill hand. But John Muir's real occupation was naturalist. In a dozen scientific fields he made first-rate findings. Species of insects, plants, and rabbits which he discovered were named after him. He became the recognized expert on Western trees, describing as never before the Douglas fir, the mountain pines, the giant sequoia. By years of painstaking research on the frozen heights, he learned the significance of glaciers in shaping the land.

Muir had a marvelous ability to "read the mountains," to piece together the record of the changing environment and its effect on living things. "Everything is flowing, going somewhere," he observed, "animals and so-called lifeless rocks as well as water."

His deepest insight was to find the inner oneness in all of nature, pointing out that "no particle is ever wasted or worn out but is eternally flowing from use to use."

Although he shunned churches, he was a man of deep reverence. A journey into the Yosemite Valley was for him a religious experience. But Muir broke with the shortsighted dogmas of his childhood. The old idea that this world is made especially for man "is not supported by the facts," he said.

"Brought into right relationship with the wilderness, man would see that he was not a separate entity endowed with a divine right to subdue his fellow creatures and destroy the common heritage but is rather an integral part of a harmonious whole," he declared. "He would see that his appropriation of earth's resources beyond his personal needs would only bring unbalance and beget ultimate loss and poverty for all."

In a time when life for most Americans was becoming more complicated, more cluttered with "things," Muir lived a life startling in its simplicity. He was poor in material goods, but "time-rich." Those who joined him on his jaunts found him a joyful man, full of deep serenity. He bathed in the spray of waterfalls, lived frugally off the land, and slept soundly in what he called "the great bedroom of the open night."

One wintry evening in the Sierra Nevada, Muir was suddenly caught in a violent storm. To his amazement the scene around him revealed a mood of nature which he had never before experienced. The wind moaned in a thousand organ voices, rising to a high wail across the craggy peaks. The mountainside seemed to be thrashing about in rage. Above the wind he heard the crashing of trees.

Here was his chance to enter a deeper realm of nature, and Muir was jubilant. Mounting a high ridge, he chose a tall spruce and began climbing to its top. As the storm grew more furious, John saw a tumultuous panorama below him. He bared all his senses to the moment, listening to the strange roaring in the treetops, viewing a landscape gone mad, breathing in air pungent with the odor of pines. The tree swung in a great arc before the wind. And, writing about his adventure later, Muir described how he clung to his lofty perch for hours, "like a bobolink on a reed." This story, like so many other exciting accounts that he wrote in 1892, was to become a part of his first book, *The Mountains of California.*

A different country

The year 1892 marked exactly four centuries since Christopher Columbus had come to the West Indies. But how different the country was from the wilderness that Columbus found! It had changed, most people thought, for the better. But many were disturbed at the scarred remains of vast forests, the ugliness of the factory towns, the misused and abandoned farm sites, the ghostly camps around emptied mines.

Some called this era "the Gay Nineties." But this was to be a decade of deep crisis among the farmers, bitter strikes in the steel and railroad industries, and a major depression, with the unemployed marching in protest across the land.

Chicago was building a World's Fair to honor Columbus's achievement—a glittering array of white palaces, in sharp contrast to the grimy districts where the city's working people lived. In the lake-front gardens of the Columbian Exposition, you could smell the reeking stockyards when the wind was right.

Foreign-born by the shipload were jamming into the cities, drawn into the coal mines around Pittsburgh, the garment sweatshops of New York City, the tanneries of St. Louis. In Alabama, a former slave named Booker T. Washington was teaching black men that the only way they could survive in America was to train themselves for industrial jobs.

In 1892 there were many new millionaires. People were more aware than ever of the widening gap between rich and poor. The writer Mark Twain had a bitter comment to make on the newly rich businessmen. "If you pick up a starving dog and make him prosperous he will not bite you," said Twain. "This is the principal difference between a dog and a man."

Rapid changes were being signaled everywhere. The newfangled automobile, filling the air with fumes and noise, clearly had come to stay. Thomas Edison, whose inventions were electrifying

America, appeared at the patent office with drawings for a motion-picture camera. Newly built blast furnaces darkened the skies of every steelmaking center. That year, river water in scores of towns became undrinkable.

In the countryside, nature seemed to strike back at every attempt of man to master the land. In 1892, Texas cotton farmers found themselves invaded by the boll weevil. Elsewhere the earth gave out, crops dwindled, the soil vanished in whirlwinds and washouts. For all the nation's new technological know-how, unforeseen troubles appeared.

On the Western plains the dwindling acres still owned by the government were being given away at a reckless rate. Land-hungry settlers lined up for a strange race to stake out claims. A signal shot rang out and the wild dash was on. In a storm of dust and flying hoofs, shrieking horsemen and wagoners charged across the plains. Within minutes farmsteads were seized. Men vied and scrambled for the level land, the watered sites, the richer soils.

Meanwhile a quieter but much bigger giveaway was going on in Washington and in the state capitals. Men with powerful influence were getting county-size plots turned over to them. The railroads got the biggest share as outright gifts. Rich mineral locations were handed out. Streams were turned over to the water-power companies. Choice timberlands went for a few cents an acre, the price of a single wooden plank.

Since the founding of the nation, the population had been doubling about every twenty-five years. The Census Bureau made another startling discovery. By the 1890s there was no longer any trace of a frontier line, no border of unsettled land. That news seemed to destroy the old myth of America's infinite abundance. The nation's resources no longer appeared boundless. Vanished was that legendary storehouse in the West where there would always be plenty of everything.

Stand up and fight

The year 1892 was also a great watershed in the life of John Muir. He had come to understand the deep hunger of people for some personal contact with unspoiled nature. For many Americans, Muir was this link. Each of his articles brought a flood of warm response from readers. And now he was finishing a book which contained a matchless description of the Western highlands.

To John Muir came the full realization that America could no longer turn back to a simple existence. The land and everything in it was being exploited at a furious rate. The natural environment which he prized was in danger. And the defensive battle for its preservation would be bitter and ceaseless. The only course was to stand up and fight with all the strength that could be mustered.

Muir had lived far from the hurly-burly of politics. But he understood now that in order to save the environment he could not remain aloof from the democratic process. He would have to speak out, organize, get into political battles, gather the sentiment of the people to influence Congress and the president. Because he was widely respected as a man of courage and wisdom, his leadership was desperately needed.

Muir had little experience in organizing for social action. But on a warm day in May, 1892, a handful of men met in a small San Francisco office. John Muir was chosen president of the organization which was formed to "enlist the support and co-operation of people and government in preserving the forests and other natural features of the Sierra Nevada Mountains." These were the beginnings of the Sierra Club which had sprung to the defense of America's remaining wilderness.

Through such efforts and through his own writings, John Muir helped to arouse the people. From the loftiest peaks of this land, he shouted in exultation for all America to hear—and thundered a warning.

"In the West, the wild gardens are sadly hacked and trampled," he wrote, "and the noblest forests are desolate and repulsive, like a face ravaged by disease.

"The same fate, sooner or later, is awaiting them all, unless awakening public opinion comes forward to stop it!"

Gifford Pinchot

Trees for Tomorrow

6. Trees for Tomorrow

For the fates of living things are bound together, and a wise man can grow wiser learning it. The perilous balance, the dangerous adventure, the thirst, the needs, the crashing end—they are impartially allotted to us all, tall man or taller tree. What we the living require is most of all each other.

Donald Culross Peattie

At times young Gifford Pinchot felt that his whole future lay simply in being a rich man's son. But by his fifteenth birthday he suddenly seemed to outgrow that idea—as he did his pants legs and shirt sleeves.

Gifford's boyhood years in the 1870s were spent on his family's vast wooded estate in Pennsylvania or in their fashionable dwellings in New York City. The boy traveled abroad. He was offered a life of luxury and ease. He could have become a country gentleman, or the wealthy prince of a business empire.

But early in life, Gifford Pinchot turned off on a rougher path. He loved the wilderness trails and the wooded countryside. When he returned from his camping trips to recount his adventures to his father, the boy's zest for the outdoors shone in his eyes. The two, father and son, agreed that Gifford's career should be forestry.

No college in America taught forestry in those days. But at

Yale, Gifford patched together a course of study that would give him the background he needed. His postgraduate work was carried on in the midst of the European forests.

In France and Germany, the young American was taught what the Europeans had learned over centuries of painful trial and error. With great care and effort, the remaining woodlands there were being safeguarded. Lumbering was carried on according to strict rules. Waste was at a minimum. Even dead brush and bundles of twigs were carefully gathered for use. Great precautions were taken against fire and blight. The forests were under the management of expert woodsmen, and these were Gifford Pinchot's teachers.

Home at last, Gifford began viewing his own country in a new light. The young Easterner, who had already seen a good part of the world, had never crossed the Allegheny Mountains to discover America. Now, at the age of 26, Pinchot went west. These early 1890s became his years of wandering and exploration. He took a close look at his native land—and at himself as well.

Trees and people

In the West, Pinchot measured his stamina against the rough frontier life. He backpacked his way into the Rockies, shared the driver's seat in a wild, jolting, all-night ride in a four-horse stagecoach, shared a haystack bed with a litter of piglets, and lived among sourdough miners, Arizona mule skinners, and Arkansas loggers. The tenderfoot gathered a few calluses.

In letters home he recounted his findings and wrote about Betsy, a case of "love at first sight." Some time later he sent his parents a photograph of himself and Betsy, a tame young Ozark bear.

The trip was an eye opener. What he observed most carefully were trees and people, and the relationship between the two. He met the frontiersman trying to carve a farm out of the backwoods. With the swing of the ax the homesteader felled the logs from which to build a cabin—and also cleared his land for pasture and crops. At the same time, he cut out fence posts and piled a supply of cordwood—also leveling the surrounding woods which might hide wild animals or enemies. What timber he didn't need for his own use, he could sell for saw logs.

What can I tell this man about preserving the woodland? the young forester wondered. How could you preach the saving of forests to men convinced that the supply was endless?

To the man with the ax, Gifford realized, a standing tree was worthless. Its value was only in its use or its sale, as log or lumber. The young forester scratched his mop of brown hair and wondered how long it would be until Americans understood the tree for its beauty and its important place in the natural setting.

What he had learned in a classroom at Yale now seemed a thousand times more clear in the woodland. Science had begun to explain the patterns of life and the arrangement of all nature into a close-meshed network of living communities. The forest is such a community. It is in fact a clustering of numerous communities—in which millions of plants and animals seek survival.

Each full-grown tree is the host for a large variety of living things. It provides them with food and shelter, and it conserves minerals among its roots and moisture in its leafy crown. A tree is an anchor for soil, a sponge for rain water, a storehouse of nature's goods. Like all other green plants, a tree emits oxygen into the atmosphere, using energy from the sun's rays. It is a life-giving thing. And the bite of an ax fells not only the tree but the entire community which it sustains.

It seemed to Gifford that America's whole future was bound up in its woodlands. A desperate and losing struggle was taking place there. The mantle of greenery had already been shredded to bits along the eastern seaboard. The hardwoods of the South had been pared away. In the Middle West, loggers were stripping the pine forests bare. It seemed only a matter of time until the towering timberlands of the West would fall.

Gifford saw the lumbermen slashing their way across the continent, leaving behind an ugly, stubbled wasteland. Lumber was a rich product, second in value only to the yield of America's farmlands. Was there any chance of stopping America's forests from being destroyed to make private fortunes?

In this growing, expanding, building nation the need for lumber was great. And Gifford had no intention of standing in the way of progress. But he saw America's lumbering practices as hopelessly shortsighted and dangerously wasteful. "Don't try to stop the ax," Pinchot counseled himself. "Just regulate its use."

Farm the woodlands

On a March morning in that year of 1891, a single sharp blow of a gavel in Congress signaled the passage of a remarkable bill, which was then quickly carried down Pennsylvania Avenue for the president's signature. A clause tacked on to the bill without debate provided that the president could set aside government lands as forest reserves. President Harrison promptly reserved thirteen million wooded acres.

Where were the agents of the lumber industry that day? Where were the lobbyists who were paid to "influence" the nation's lawmakers by every honest and dishonest means? Were they caught napping by those few sentences which were to save miles of timberland from the ax and the sawmill?

In time the reserved forests would include timbered tracts across the West, as well as vast pineries in the Gulf states, maple forests in New England, tall stands of evergreens in the Great Lakes region. In years to come the reserved woodlands would become known as Sequoia and Cibola, Medicine Bow and Arapaho, Bitterroot and Beaverhead. Almost every president would add to what later became known as the national forests.

However, the new reserves of 1891 were reserves in name only. Unfenced and unguarded, they were soon being used by a variety of trespassers. Stockmen drove in their grazing herds. Squatters moved in. Mining, water-power, and oil interests raided the federal woodlands. The cry of the day was "Free enterprise!" and, in the spirit of the times, men used that slogan to grab whatever they could get.

Some of the lumbermen helped themselves. They simply stole publicly owned timber, openly logging and milling it, sometimes even selling the finished lumber back to the United States government at a high price!

Gifford, the rich man's son, was appalled at how these rich

men were getting richer. In his diary he confessed his anger at "the exploiters, pushing farther and farther into the wilderness." Many had no real interest in building America. They were simply out to invest their money so that it doubled itself every few years.

Young Pinchot looked on his homeland with worry in his eyes. He saw how rapidly America was being stripped of its natural heritage and wondered about his own part in saving it. As a forester, he tried to view America with the woodsman's eye—seeing both the forest and the trees.

It was clear to him now that he would never succeed simply by preaching his beliefs. He would have to prove that scientific forestry was practical—and profitable. In a sudden flash of insight he realized that his best course was to put his ideas into practice in the woods. He could then show by example that a well-managed timber stand could be made to produce a substantial annual yield, without destroying the forest itself.

Yes, the nation could be taught to "farm" its woodlands. Gifford was sure of that. Long-range planning and careful lumbering practices could produce crop after crop endlessly. America could use its forests—and have them too!

Science in the forest

Astride a mule, the gangling, hawk-faced youth made his way across the North Carolina uplands. At the place where he paused to stretch his legs stood a cabin, its fence enclosing a tombstone.

Young Gifford Pinchot would not long remember the name of the man who was buried there. But he was never to forget the words on the grave marker: "He left this country better than he found it." For a lifetime Pinchot would work tirelessly to deserve such an epitaph.

By dusk that spring evening, Gifford was camped in a pine

grove. The young forester was now in charge of a private woodland owned by the wealthy Vanderbilt family. Here he was free to plan and carry out a systematic program of forestry.

The previous autumn he had been in this same stand of giant pines, supervising a crew of loggers. Gifford had selected and marked the full-grown trees for cutting. While the axes thudded, Pinchot had busied himself planting the new growth which would someday replace the felled giants.

Now returned after some months, the forester was inspecting his project. The section of timber had been carefully thinned out, the oldest trees cut down and carried away on a logging road. In the openings stood the frail and spindly newcomers, growing in the shadowy corridors of an ancient mountain greenland. Around the newly planted sprouts stood the hundred-footers, straight-boled and majestic.

In the darkling woods, Gifford knelt on the mossy mat of the forest floor. His seedlings were doing well. Some would not survive. The healthier ones had reached their own sources of sunlight and moisture; they would come along fine. Not in a year or even ten, but in time they too would be towering shafts piercing the mountain sky.

This was an exciting time for the young forester. He was testing his own ideas. At stake were his hopes for the future, the example he was trying to set for forestry in America.

From between his blankets that night, Gifford Pinchot glimpsed a star among the piny crowns. Cold, fresh wind stirred the mountain air. The young forester was tired but sleepless, his mind full of momentous questions.

Could this be the beginning of a new life for this country's woodlands? Had the time come when the nation would stop destroying its green heritage? And was it possible that America's scientific forestry had at last begun here in this unmarked grove? The questions were too big for easy answers. It was far too early to predict the outcome of the struggle to which the young forester had zealously dedicated his life.

Save or use?

He was a young man in a feverish haste those next years, burning with a message, caught up in the cause of scientific forestry. Gifford traveled about seeking allies in his campaign, occasionally winning supporters for his point of view. But the lumbermen he met looked upon him as a woolly-minded young dreamer. They saw no need for new theories in a hard-driving industry, long operated on a simple routine: Chop and haul, saw and sell.

On a Pacific coast trip, Gifford met the naturalist who had become a legend in the Western woodlands—John Muir. The white-bearded Muir and the youthful Pinchot spent the late September days together in the canyon country, filling themselves with the spectacular scenic beauty of the region.

At one campsite, they suddenly noticed a scorpion poised on a log. Gifford instantly lifted a rock and took aim. But Muir raised his hand, saying, "It has as much right here as we have." The younger man realized that Muir felt the same way about killing a scorpion as he did about plucking a flower or felling a tree.

The icy wind sang through the nut-pine and cedar woods as the two camped on the rim of the Grand Canyon. They sat up late beside the campfire in the cold, starlit night. Muir was a poet and a superb storyteller—and Gifford listened.

The young forester was inspired by Muir's feeling of oneness with all of nature. But sadly Gifford realized that the differences in their thinking were as deep as the chasm spreading out below them. Muir believed in keeping nature pure and untouched, holding a firm line against the invasions of man. Pinchot favored the development of America and the best use of its resources. In time their views would spread even wider apart. The key to

Muir's beliefs was in the word "Save!" Pinchot's watchword was "Use!"

Chief forester

Increasingly, Gifford was hearing the call from the Capitol to bring his knowledge and his talents into the government service. Pine-tall and rugged, packed with energy and plans, Pinchot strode into Washington on a sultry June day in 1898. He found his new office in the Department of Agriculture musty and cramped. But his title was as big as the outdoors. He was Gifford Pinchot, United States Forester.

Gifford soon became a familiar figure, speeding around Washington on a bicycle, his long mustache flowing in the wind. Quickly he learned what he called "the game of government." It was, in fact, a game of skill, teamwork, cunning—and sometimes chance.

In a short time Pinchot was being pointed out as a tireless and effective public servant. In an era when corruption, theft, and the selling of favors were widespread among government employees, Pinchot was a crusader for strict honesty. His bureau proved to be stainless. He was, moreover, an extraordinary leader of men and an excellent manager.

The tiny office in Washington saw little of him. Restless and active, he spent a great deal of time out in the field, in the timberlands. He also made contacts with those men in the federal and state governments who would help him achieve his goals.

On a trip into the Adirondacks, Pinchot stopped at the New York capital, Albany, to see the governor, Theodore Roosevelt. When he arrived at the mansion the chief executive was lowering his children with ropes out the upper windows in a game of make-believe which all were enjoying. Gifford joined briefly in the fun.

Roosevelt, or T.R., as he was called, seemed to do everything with great zest. A weakling as a boy, Roosevelt had built himself through strenuous exercise and sports into a vigorous outdoorsman.

The forester and the governor quickly hit it off well together. They rode horses the following morning in the cold rain. Later they tossed a medicine ball in the governor's well-fitted gymnasium. A young bull of a man, T.R. quickly pinned his visitor to the mat in a wrestling match. At boxing, Pinchot threw a long punch that knocked the governor off his sturdy legs. With apologies, Pinchot knelt quickly to help. Roosevelt responded with a toothy grin, then burst into high-pitched laughter and bounded to his feet.

That afternoon the two men took a long mountain climb together, discussing forestry and the safeguarding of one of the nation's most valuable resources. Roosevelt was in full agreement with Pinchot's ideas.

In his own state the governor was vigorously battling the big lumber interests who were turning the forests of upper New York into a shambles. He asked the chief forester to suggest plans of action.

Gifford was pleased when T.R.'s annual address to the state legislature contained the forester's main ideas, strongly stated. "We need to have our system of forestry gradually developed and conducted along scientific principles," declared Roosevelt. "Unrestrained greed means the ruin of the great woods and the drying up of the sources of the rivers."

New hope

A new century was dawning. And suddenly Gifford Pinchot was filled with real hope for America's future. He knew now that his voice was no longer a lone outcry in the silent wilderness.

Pinchot realized how much could be accomplished in working with a man like Theodore Roosevelt as governor. The two, Gifford and T.R., became even closer friends later that year when Roosevelt was elected vice-president of the United States.

Pinchot was now finding new support for his ideas here and there. But the problems of the timberlands were nationwide in scope. And the government in Washington seemed to lack a clear policy for dealing effectively with the need in all parts of the country. Gifford found himself caught in a cross fire of regional differences and jealousies.

The Civil War, which had ended in the year Gifford Pinchot was born, had arrayed North against South. In the clashes of the 1890s it was often East against West. The eastern seaboard, with its powerful banks, railroads, and industrial centers, was driving headlong into the twentieth century. Eagerly Westerners sought to grasp their share of riches—and to do so in their own free style. They balked at anything that smacked of control or plan. They wanted no rules to slow them down or laws to restrict their actions.

As they saw it, they had won the West. They had fought off the Indians, the storms, and the beasts. And no Eastern dude with an official title would tell them what to do!

Gifford Pinchot, United States Forester, represented everything hateful. He was an Easterner born and bred. A member of a wealthy family, Pinchot was college-educated and trained in Europe. Highfalutin, they called him, a stuffed shirt, full of opinions about how the West should be run.

However, Gifford was not one to back off from these unfriendly attitudes. As the nation's top man in the field, he knew that the most crucial forestry problems were in the West. The ruthless cutting of the timberlands there was playing havoc with the delicate balance between vegetation, water, and soil. In the wake of careless logging came devastating forest fires. Heavy grazing of livestock, especially sheep, was killing off the green cover, and the earth was being pounded brick-hard by herds too large for the ranges. The soil of the arid regions, sliced up by the plow, became parched and dusty through the long dry spells. When the rains came at last, they washed rapidly over the barren slopes, and the topsoil went sliding into the rivers. We were winning the West, but losing its resources!

Sound of trumpets

On a rainy September night in 1901, a mountaineer reached Vice-president Theodore Roosevelt, who was camped on a high peak in the Adirondacks. Breathless, the messenger gasped the news that President McKinley had been shot and was dying.

Roosevelt lost no time in getting down the mountainside. Changing to fresh horses as he rode, T.R. clattered through the night across New York State to reach McKinley's bedside in Buffalo. Within days, the president was dead. By a strange turn of chance, an assassin's bullet had suddenly thrust Theodore Roosevelt into the White House.

As the youngest president America had ever had, Roosevelt brought a new spirit into stuffy, officious Washington. On his morning hikes across the town, he was accompanied by a group of close co-workers who matched the president's athletic style, Pinchot among them. Often the early exercise began with a rugged climb in nearby Rock Creek Park.

On a freezing November morning T.R.'s little party came to the edge of a swamp, which blocked their line of march. Undaunted, the chief executive waded in. Pinchot and the others followed. One striped-pants diplomat from the State Department discovered halfway across that he was still carrying his umbrella. "A lot of good this is doing me now!" he cried out, his teeth chattering.

Grinning like a mischievous brat, Gifford arrived home that morning muddy and dripping. A Pinchot family servant, who had been his nursemaid as a child, took one dismayed look at him and scolded: "You've been out with the president!"

From the start Theodore Roosevelt made it clear that his administration would be on patrol to protect the land, its minerals, agriculture, woodlands, and streams.

"Whatever destroys the forest," warned the president in his opening message to Congress, "threatens our well-being." The words sounded in the Capitol like a fanfare of trumpets.

With Gifford Pinchot at his side, the new chief executive announced a fighting program. Open war was declared on "the land thieves," the looters of the public domain. In words that crackled with anger, Roosevelt vowed that he would not stand by and watch the amassing of huge private fortunes at the expense of America and its people.

Pinchot was now a part of the first-string White House team, a member of what came to be known as the Tennis Cabinet. These were associates of President Roosevelt who not only shared his enjoyment of the strenuous outdoor activity but also advised him in matters of policy.

Often Pinchot was in the executive mansion long before the regular working day began, discussing problems with the president while the White House barber gave T.R. his morning shave. At dusk the two could often be found finishing a vigorous set of tennis.

Pinchot was impatient with the progress of forestry. As things stood, the Department of the Interior administered all the public forests, but it had no foresters on its staff. All the government's trained foresters were in the Department of Agriculture—which had no forests under its care. Forests and foresters were securely locked away from each other.

Roosevelt asked Congress to transfer the federal timberlands to the Department of Agriculture. But the lumber lobby would not be caught napping again. It repeatedly lined up the votes in Congress to keep the reserves from falling under Pinchot's care.

Meanwhile, the chief forester was limited to giving out free advice to whoever would take it. He answered letters from landscape gardeners. A forceful speaker, Gifford appeared before any group that would listen. He issued pamphlets on the proper management of forests. He even offered to send his men to give technical assistance to the lumber industry. But he had few takers. His big moment came on February 1, 1905.

The rangers

In the White House, President Roosevelt had before him the long-delayed bill which had finally been passed. It provided for the transfer of the federal forest reserves to the Department of Agriculture. With a triumphant flourish of his pen, Roosevelt turned over to Pinchot's bureau 86 million acres of woodland—an area three times the size of the state of Pennsylvania. Before he was out of office, T.R. would double the acreage of the federal forests.

The wealthy lumbermen and their friends in Congress continued to battle the Roosevelt administration every inch of the way. They tried to blame the administration for the high price of lumber, charging that this was due to the official policy of reserving more and more timberlands. The states fought bitterly against the federal withdrawal of newly reserved lands from their jurisdiction. A hot-tempered Western senator arose in Congress. "What little remains of Idaho," he shouted, "will fight!"

To patrol the forests Pinchot carefully built a corps of outstanding hand-picked men—the rangers. These were young foresters devoted to a life in the woodlands. Many of them came fresh and high-spirited out of the newly established forestry schools. They were thoroughly trained for their new jobs and had to pass a rigorous series of tests. For the tenderfoot, often the most trying part of the exam was: "1) Cook a meal in the outdoors. 2) Eat it!"

Under Pinchot's personal attention the rangers became a famed body of men, skilled and fearless. They distinguished themselves as brave fire fighters. Often facing danger and hardship, they became the protectors of plant and animal life in the wilds. At times they acted as peacemakers in the violent range wars between the stockmen and the homesteaders. Courageously they stood up against the big lumber interests, enforcing Pinchot's forestry rules to halt the abuse and waste of the government's timberlands.

Gifford and his men patiently tried to explain the value of improved lumbering methods, of forestry as "tree farming." Across the arid West the rangers pleaded that the forests be saved in order to preserve precious water supplies. They showed how the woods absorb rainfall, check the runoff, hold back the erosion of the soil, slow down the melting of snows, reduce the spring floods, and save up water for the dry months of summer.

An age of reform

A new spirit of reform was reaching widely into many areas of American life in the Theodore Roosevelt period. This was a time of public awakening, an upsurge of anger and action.

A peaceful rebellion was growing against the worsening conditions of life. Above all, this was a movement in behalf of children. The outcry began in the cities, where a dark blight shadowed the lives of hundreds of thousands who were to be the nation's hope for the future. Common childhood diseases were taking a high toll. In the factory and mining towns, half-grown boys and girls labored long hours under unsafe and unhealthy conditions.

Social workers, welfare agencies, and labor unions joined in a crusade to save the children. Against the bitter opposition of factory owners, new laws were proposed to take the children out of the factories and put them into schools. Even though the slums and the ghettoes remained, a series of reforms in public health, education, recreation, and child welfare brought definite improvements. Strong campaigns favored an eight-hour working day, women's voting rights, and taxes based on the principle that the largest share should come from those best able to pay.

Roosevelt and his Progressive movement played a leading part in these efforts. At the polls, the voters in those years swept out many corrupt officials. Some of the most brazen of the land grabs were exposed and the guilty sent to jail. In his fight to halt the wildfire of greed and waste that was ravaging the nation's resources, the president depended strongly on his forester. Pinchot's speeches rang with powerful accusations against those who were "robbing the future."

Gaunt and long-boned, Pinchot was a striking figure as he toured the country. His appearance was impressive—the pointed mustache, the sharply cut features under a broad-brimmed hat.

For all his zeal and hard work, however, Pinchot fell short of his own goals and hopes. Forestry was definitely changing. He could dimly foresee a time when the yearly harvest of timber would be no greater than the amount of new growth. But America was still cutting six trees for every one planted.

A battle cry

Late one February day in 1907, Gifford Pinchot was a lone horseman in a wooded park near the Capitol. As he rode, the forester's mind groped for an idea. He seemed to be close to some symbol or slogan that would catch the bright new spirit of the age.

Streaky, dun-colored clouds were being driven by a high wind. As the weak sun burned off the haze, a strange brightness glowed in the sky.

An idea, an image, a word—what was it? Pinchot reached for some way to express the full scope not only of forestry but of the entire nation's surge to save its rich national heritage and its beauty. How, in a word, could he describe the deep-felt need of the people to protect the very earth on which man's life depends?

Reserve, preserve, conserve? Yes, that was it! The tall figure in the saddle bent over his mount. He slapped the colt's flank and gave him the signal for flight. "Go, Jim, let's go!" The hoofs thundered across the turf.

Conservation! The one word seemed to draw all the separate pieces into one great central need—to use the earth for the good of man. This planet was the source of life. What could be more important for man than to conserve the resources which make life possible?

Conservation! The word was to become a battle cry, an ideal, a movement, a crusade. Conservation was also to become a confusing label attached to conflicting ideas and goals.

But in the early years of the century conservation swept across America like a fresh wind. The nation seemed to be coming of age. People felt a new responsibility for what was happening to the entire country.

The nine years of the Roosevelt–Pinchot era were coming to an end. The two men tried at last to direct the nation's thinking and action toward future programs that would carry the conservation effort to greater heights. Hard experience had proved to them that country and city problems, soils and minerals, forests and food, were all linked together. No piecemeal plan was broad enough. These resources were in turn centered around the large water basins and the watersheds of America.

"The time has come," urged Theodore Roosevelt, in a report prepared by Pinchot, "for merging local projects and uses of the inland waters in a comprehensive plan designed to benefit the entire country."

But such bold planning was for another day in a later decade. The expanded program had to wait for another Roosevelt in the White House—and for a new guardian of America's resources with the courage and foresight of Gifford Pinchot.

George W. Norris

Troubled Waters

7. Troubled Waters

Though you drive Nature out with a pitchfork, she will still find her way back.

Horace

As some men worry about money, so George W. Norris worried about water.

In his farming years he had seen dust in the bottom of his well and spring floods flowing wild across his fresh-plowed fields. Water was a maker of human environments; Norris knew that from experience. Through the late years of his life he would be a storm center among men fighting fiercely for the control of water and water power.

His earliest memories were of the harsh life on a poor, small farm in Ohio. There he came to know the meaning of water, of too much or too little. Young George had hauled it endlessly, until the bucket handles left deep welts in his palms. On his knees he had prayed in fear to halt the rising of the river. He knew the taste of pure, cold water in his parched throat and the miracle of rain on a thirsty land.

Within a single dark year, George's only brother was killed on a Civil War battlefield and his father died on the farm. Fatherless at the age of three, the boy took on a man's work early in life, helping his mother and sisters run the farm.

To George the farm was like a sick calf bawling loudly for attention every hour of the day and a good part of the night. Working hard and living frugally, the family survived lean years. Mrs. Norris managed well and planned for her children an education and a better life.

On a late summer day in 1877, George William Norris and his two sisters arrived at a plain little college in Berea, Ohio. It was known as a "poor man's school," and the Norris trio were about as moneyless as any of its other students.

George was a sturdy young fellow, with hands callused by chores and arms tough as ax handles. The three found an attic in town in which to live. While the two girls kept house, the boy hired himself out at odd jobs to pay the tuition. All three did well at their studies. And George went on to take up law.

A senator's riddle

The closing years of the century found Norris out in Nebraska. As a struggling rural lawyer in a threadbare suit, his livelihood rose and fell with the crops. Later, as a county judge, he gave every benefit of the law to the small farmer beset by drought and debt, insects and mortgage bankers.

In 1902 he was elected to Congress. For the next forty years he would be the representative of the common man in Washington. He never lost touch with the plain workingman or the dirt farmer. It was his lifelong farmer's habit to scan the sky daily for a rain cloud and lift his hand to feel the dryness of the wind.

Norris was a mild, quiet man who took his work in Congress seriously. His style was not that of flowing oratory or straining to make newspaper headlines. He was a Republican supporter of Theodore Roosevelt during the years of T.R.'s conservation crusade, and he backed the movement to save America's resources.

By 1917 the war raging across Europe was slowly drawing the United States into its fiery midst. To Norris, it was clear that the American people had no stake in that war. He knew, however, of the heavy financial interest of many large United States corporations in the Allied cause. Norris, now a senator, had so far drawn little national attention. But the Senate chamber suddenly went silent when the Nebraskan arose during the war debate.

"War brings prosperity," declared Senator Norris, "to those who are already in possession of more wealth than can be realized or enjoyed." As for himself, the senator was more concerned about "human suffering and the sacrifice of human life."

But the flags were flying and America was caught up in a patriotic fever. The newspapers took up a shrill cry against Norris and a tiny group of congressmen who voted with him against United States entry into the war.

Norris's attention was drawn to a section of the Tennessee River known as Muscle Shoals. Ancient Indian tribes had found here a bounty of shellfish, and the name of the rapids came from its fresh-water mussels, in misspelled form.

These white-water cascades, filled with flinty rocks, were the funnel of one of America's mightiest rivers. Throughout the nineteenth century, many vain attempts had been made to provide a way for river traffic to by-pass this troublesome barrier. By the twentieth century, however, Muscle Shoals was suddenly recognized as a valuable source of hydroelectric power.

As part of the immense war effort of 1917, a giant dam and two large chemical plants were built by the federal government at Muscle Shoals. The dam was to furnish power for the making of nitrates, used in explosives.

With the end of the war, Muscle Shoals became the special problem of Senator George W. Norris, who headed the Senate committee in charge of this project. The dam and the plants were now idle. In the Capitol, the senator from Red Willow County, Nebraska, pondered some bewildering facts.

Oddly, the nitrates which were so important in war were also useful in making fertilizer. It seemed clear to Norris that the Muscle Shoals project should be reopened by the government to produce electrical power and fertilizer. Both were much in demand by the farmers of the Tennessee Valley. In fact, the potential products of Muscle Shoals and the regional need for them seemed to fit together like lock and key.

But no! Things didn't seem to work quite that way. And with a grim little smile, Senator Norris explained the irony of it to his colleagues.

During wartime the government was free to expend money and manpower on almost any enterprise. But once the emergency was over, there were strong objections against "government in business," for whatever purpose. If the energies of the nation and its wealth were available for war, Senator Norris wanted to know, why couldn't the same public resources be used to solve the urgent problems of the people in peacetime?

A rebel's way

By asking this kind of question Senator Norris had already won himself a reputation as a rebel. The senator had drawn the bitter hatred of those large business firms which had profited greatly in World War I. He was as troublesome as a nettle to the mighty water-power interests, blocking every effort they made to seize control of Muscle Shoals.

In Congress he defied the leaders of both political parties. Following his own beliefs on issues, the Nebraskan refused to vote as he was instructed. His own party leaders had long since turned their backs on him. Firm in his independence, Norris followed a difficult path. There were few legislative victories for him in these years.

In July, 1921, Norris celebrated his sixtieth birthday. He was getting tired now, feeling not only his age but also the weariness of the uphill battle in Congress. In fact, he had begun to talk to friends about his retirement.

But that day shocking news came for Norris from Muscle Shoals. A new attempt was being made to grab the government project. This time it was Henry Ford, the noted automobile manufacturer. Ford was now selling more than a million motor cars a year. The low-cost, mass-produced "Tin Lizzies" were sputtering their way across a nation rapidly becoming motorized.

In a bold move to enlarge his industrial holdings, Henry Ford offered to take over Muscle Shoals at a small fraction of its original cost. The deal would give Ford not only the Wilson Dam and the two chemical plants but also two villages, several thousand acres of land, a short-line railroad, several other plants, and a quarry.

"I have seen the people defeated time and again," Norris told reporters, "and I think they are about to be hornswoggled again."

However, the senator was not giving up the battle. The public had paid a lot of money for Muscle Shoals, he declared, and the public was entitled to the benefits from it. Norris was angry and determined. Instead of retiring, the Nebraskan quickly forgot his backaches and his heartaches and plunged into a fight.

At that moment, still another attempt was being made to plunder the public domain. The key figure in the conspiracy was a cabinet member named Albert B. Fall. Even though he was an outspoken foe of conservation, President Harding had made him Secretary of the Interior and placed him in charge of vast public resources.

As the scandal slowly came to light, it was shown that Fall had received large sums of money, supposedly as "loans" and "gifts" from wealthy men who represented large American oil companies. In return, Fall had turned over to them the use of government-owned oilfields at a tableland region known as Teapot Dome, Wyoming, and others at Elk Hills, California. Together with a group of his close friends in the Senate, Norris dug into this oily mess. At the same time, the Nebraskan fought off the giveaway at Muscle Shoals. To him, that was an attempted raid "so great that it makes Teapot Dome look like a pinhead."

The electrical age

Senator Norris now was a man with a mission. He saw it as his duty to awaken the American people to the slow and steady loss of their storehouse of riches.

But these were strange times. The 1920s were a heedless decade. The wealthy were adding to their fortunes at a dizzying pace. For most working people there was employment, some making what they considered good wages. The middle classes were enjoying a soothing kind of prosperity. Few people could be aroused to the signs of danger.

What if strip mining was leaving ugly scars on the land? Who cared if the junk heaps of discarded autos were piling up mountain-high? Why worry if the chemicals pouring from the factory chimneys were poisoning the air and killing off the plant life for miles around? Whose concern was it that towns at the water's edge were filling their rivers and lakes with waste matter? All these seemed to be by-products of "progress."

There were new things called radio and rayon to think about. Gushers in Oklahoma were spouting crude oil skyward. Property values were booming in Florida. Skyscrapers were outclimbing one another in the cities. This was the new day of the chain store and the gilded movie palace. The stock market was going up and up, out of sight. A new industry flourished, called advertising— and in the 1920s it persuaded millions of Americans to chew gum, smoke cigarettes, and drive late-model cars.

Senator Norris liked to think of this as "the electrical age," lighting up the nation, lightening the drudgery of the people. He remembered his own boyhood and his numb fingers on the bitter-cold mornings when he milked the cows by the light of a tallow candle. But now electricity was a glowing reality at last. And yet, so much of rural America still lay deep in a darker age.

Cheap electric power, available to all—this was the senator's dream. But in his opinion, giant corporations stood between the people and the light-giving water-power resources of this country.

"Every stream in the United States which flows from the mountains through the meadows to the sea has the possibility of producing electricity for cheap power and cheap lighting to be carried into the homes and businesses and industry of the American people," Norris pointed out. "No man and no organization of men ought to be allowed to make a financial profit out of it."

In his angriest moments the senator cried out against "the power trust." He knew now that this was the enemy in his long fight to set into motion the government project at Muscle Shoals. The private electrical utilities were determined either to wrest it from the public or to make sure that the government power plant never turned a wheel. Senator Norris sensed bitterly his own failure in combating these shadowy forces that stood in the way.

The senator was now a frequent visitor to the Tennessee Valley. Some three million people lived in a great basin edged by the crestlines of the Blue Ridge Mountains, the Great Smokies, and the southern Appalachians. Rain water and melt water drained down through a seven-state region by way of rivulets, upland streams, and broadening tributaries into the mighty river.

Mud or flood

The Tennessee was a dozen rivers in one. Its moods changed at each level of altitude and at every season of the year. The late summer turned it sluggish, and in places the channel dried to a trickle. By springtime, strength gathered in the mountains carried the river swirling westward past cities and farmlands, until it churned its way through Muscle Shoals and went on to join the Ohio River less than fifty miles from where the Ohio reaches the Mississippi.

Life-giving moisture coursed down through the Tennessee Valley. But the river held danger as well. Periodically it overswelled its banks to go raging across the land. Crop fields and homesteads were swept away in its tides. Riverside towns were left in ruins. In Knoxville and Chattanooga people learned never to ignore the force of nature, even in the steel-and-stone structure of a large city. Repeatedly the Tennessee River came in to remind them how flimsy were their dikes, their buildings, their man-made patterns of life.

The Tennessee Valley was one great pocket of poverty. Even during the prosperous years of the 1920s, this was a region of depressed people. Senator Norris found here an endless dreary stretch of warped shacks and washed-out roads, overcut forests and overused land. The hill folk were themselves the mirror image of the rutted slopes, the seedy towns, the wasted farms.

Their forebears had pioneered here in a green wilderness. But something had happened in the course of several generations. The countryside had simply gone sour, like stale milk. An environment friendly to man had become hostile.

Senator Norris was struck with the way people's lives can be broken down by natural conditions that are running downhill. There was the same worn-out look in the soil as in the faces of the hill people. Haunted by fear and famine, they had given up faith in the land. As for the river, winding down from the peaks, they were wary of it; tame today, it might turn savage tomorrow.

"That river has only two stages," people said, "either mud or flood!"

Many of the resources of the region had vanished. Earlier, eager-eyed men had come through, helped themselves to treasures, then moved on. Back in the woods there were still great sawdust mounds where lumbermen had cleaned out the valuable hardwoods. Minerals had been taken out as well. At Ducktown,

Tennessee, one company mined a vein of copper. In the smeltery they built, the furnaces were fired with the hardwood which they stripped from the region's forests. The sulfur fumes then destroyed the rest of the vegetation. Across the barren earth the rain water cut deep ravines, leaving the entire area a blackened, hideous wasteland.

Most damaging of all to the entire river valley was the destruction of the soil. On the tiny farms, many operated by black or white sharecroppers, the soil had been abused by the farmers' desperate need to make a cash crop. Year after year the farms were repeatedly planted with cotton, corn, or tobacco. The land suffered from its treatment at the hands of men who were both poor and ill-informed. Forests that might have held valuable moisture were cut away. On the slopes the water coursed down through the crop furrows, carrying the topsoil down into the river. The land needed a rest. But there was no hoard of food to fill the gap through a fallow season. Nor was there money for fertilizer.

The broad outlines of the problem with which Senator Norris was dealing were now becoming clear. To him it was no longer simply a matter of operating a single dam or fertilizer plant. This was a vast human environment in serious trouble. Why not respond to it with an answer of the same huge size and scope?

A law of nature

The senator hurried back to Washington for a new try at writing a Muscle Shoals bill, at winning congressional votes in the only way he knew—by simple, reasonable argument of the facts. Norris stayed out of the dealing and trading that went on behind the scenes in Washington. He wanted no political favors and gave none. He shunned the gay parties and the bright social life in the capital. In all his years in office, he never owned any formal clothes. "Stiff shirts and high collars with spike-tail coats," he said, "all cover up and conceal the real man."

The dark suit and black string tie expressed Senator Norris's plainness and simplicity. His clothes were old-fashioned. But as he grew older, the mind of George W. Norris groped for the newest of ideas. For many of them he earned much abuse. He had little trouble making his ideas clear to working men and women, to the Nebraska farm folk or to the Tennessee hill people. But to others he appeared as either a hardened radical or an impractical dreamer. His efforts at Muscle Shoals were often compared to the experiments at government economic planning which were then being tried in the Soviet Union. One congressman charged that Norris was trying to "graft our American system on to the Russian idea." This mild, aged man was actually accused of trying to become a dictator.

Senator Norris replied to these attacks with quiet dignity. "The danger of dictatorship arises," he said, "when those who toil on the farm, in the workshop, and in the counting houses are overburdened and bowed down with injustice at the hands of those who control the property of the nation."

The Nebraskan was not afraid of federal operation of any enterprise—"if the government can do it better than anybody else."

By stubborn and patient effort, Senator Norris twice managed to get a Muscle Shoals bill approved by Congress. But President Coolidge vetoed one bill, and three years later President Hoover vetoed the second. Hoover appeared horrified at the thought of the government's operating the Muscle Shoals plants. He feared, he said, that this would "break down the initiative and enterprise of the American people."

But from what Senator Norris could see, the farmers of the Tennessee Valley were broken in spirit—long before any government programs were set into operation. He came to know the region's farmer and his problems as did no other official in Washington. The man he found in these hills was of pioneer stock, reared in the old-fashioned ideals of self-reliance, liberty, and independence. However, something had gone wrong here with the idea that all a man needed in America was his rugged individualism and the free-enterprise system. The valley farmer that Senator Norris knew was the victim of grinding poverty, which had destroyed his pride and ambition. He lived in an environment which was no longer livable. It had changed completely since his ancestors came here with Daniel Boone and Davy Crockett.

He could not give his children anything better to eat than corn pone and sowbelly. Nor had they shoes to wear to the run-down school in the region. Plumbing and sanitation were lacking. He and his family were weak from lack of good food and sick with malaria and hookworm. On his farm this settler fought drought and flood, corn borers and boll weevils. The only horsepower he knew was that of an underfed mule. His chief crop was trouble—and a plentiful yield of it.

Senator Norris's long experience had taught him that a pattern of life links everything together—whether on a single farm, in a river valley, or in an entire nation. Thinking of the poverty he saw in the Tennessee basin, Norris pointed out to his fellow congressmen: "It is a law of nature that one portion of the country cannot permanently and properly and honestly be prosperous and happy while other great portions of the country are in distress and suffering from lack of the necessaries of life."

This white-haired old man was no prophet. But America would soon have occasion to recall his words.

Boom and bust

In late October 1929, a shattering blow was felt across the land. The stock market burst like an overblown toy balloon. Puffed-up values of goods, real estate, and securities suddenly went limp. Within months, the swollen prosperity had completely fizzled out. Banking, commerce, and industry grew weak. An eerie silence spread across Brooklyn's shipyards, Gary's steel mills, San Francisco's docks, Detroit's auto plants.

Many a boom in America had ended in a bust. But none had ever been like this one. Almost half the wage earners in the nation had no steady pay. Farmers, with no buyers for their produce, were being turned out of their homesteads. The unemployed prowled the dark city streets. The American who cherished his independence was to learn how interdependent was the entire nation.

When Senator Norris returned home from Congress the following summer, angry clouds were rolling across the great plains. Dust storms were a somber symbol of the nation's crisis. In his home town, groups of anxious, fearful neighbors clustered around Norris. "What's going to happen?" they wanted to know. "What is the government doing?" Grim-faced, the senator told them the harsh truth. The Hoover administration had virtually folded its hands, convinced that the trouble would soon blow over. Norris said that congressmen like himself, eager to take vigorous action, were a powerless handful.

Moreover, Norris was not sure he would be returned to his Senate seat. An election was coming up and the big water-power interests were out to defeat him at all costs. Top leaders of his own party were already moving behind the scenes to ensure the defeat of George W. Norris.

The scheme they hit upon filled them with glee at their own cleverness. In the little Nebraska town of Broken Bow, they located a grocery clerk who was persuaded, for a small amount of money, to run for the United States Senate. His name happened to be George W. Norris.

The trick was simple. Three names would appear on the ballot, two of them identical. It would be impossible for either George W. Norris to win. The crafty planners of this fraud counted on an easy victory for the third candidate, who was really their choice.

However, the schemers failed to reckon with the anger of the Nebraska voters, once they had learned of this hoax. Nor did they realize how much fighting spirit they had aroused in the aged Senator Norris.

By election day the scheme was exposed and thrown out by the courts. Grocer George's name was barred from the ballot. The real George W. Norris won re-election by a large vote.

Two years later came a national election, which swept a new administration into Washington. Winning the presidency in the midst of a paralyzing national crisis, Franklin D. Roosevelt quickly prepared for a series of bold moves to get the country moving again.

In the speeches of the new Roosevelt, Senator Norris heard a strong echo of an earlier Roosevelt. F.D.R., as he came to be known, was a lifelong Democrat. But like his Republican cousin, Theodore Roosevelt, he was deeply committed to the struggle to save the resources of the nation. He too was a stanch conservationist, openly opposed to the despoilers of America.

Another Roosevelt

Hardly were the election results in when president-elect Roosevelt asked Norris to join him on a trip. In mid-January, 1933, F.D.R. and the Nebraska senator stood on the high bluff overlooking Muscle Shoals. The huge, idle Wilson Dam stood astride the river, and the two men watched the surge of the foaming water through the spillway.

Deep within the dam hung a rusty water wheel. The president-elect fully understood Norris's deep desire to set that great wheel humming again.

For Roosevelt, the gigantic task ahead would be to set the whole American system back into motion. He would be choosing carefully those wheels which would in turn move other drive wheels of this country's economy, linked to a whole chain of pulleys and pivots, gears and axles—in order to end the deadly idleness of the nation.

Roosevelt and Norris spent time together in the sun, noting the signs of an early spring. Coming from such totally different backgrounds, the two men found an amazingly close kinship. Poor farm boy and rich heir of a well-to-do family, they had both grown up with a deep love of nature.

As a youngster Roosevelt had found that his family's acres at Hyde Park, New York, had "just plain given out," depleted by generations of one-crop farming, its soil too poor to be farmed any longer. Young Roosevelt set to work planting thousands of trees there. He told of his hope "that my grandchildren will be able to try raising corn again—just one century from now."

The president's words brought back to Norris's mind a matching story from his own childhood. As a young boy, George Norris helped his mother one day as she strained to plant a small fruit tree. It seemed to him a useless waste of heavy toil, since ailing Mrs. Norris might never live long enough to see the tree bear fruit. The boy voiced his thoughts.

"I may never see this tree in bearing, son," his mother replied, "but somebody will."

As Roosevelt and Norris talked about what was ahead for America, they found a common point of view. Both of them seemed to couple their sense of the nation's long-range needs with a strong urge to act on the problems of the moment.

Roosevelt had already made up his mind about two things. "The first," he said, "is to put Muscle Shoals to work." Secondly, F.D.R. had plans for a great development of the entire river valley.

Back in Washington, Norris was asked by newsmen for his impression of the man who was about to enter the White House.

"Do you think you can work with him?" they wanted to know. "Is he really with you?"

"He is more than with me," the Nebraskan replied with a broad smile. "He plans to go even farther than I did."

The next months saw history unfold and an immense program of government action take shape. In what became known as the New Deal, a far-reaching series of laws was enacted by Congress in the first hundred days of the Roosevelt administration. High on the list of new legislation was the Norris bill to establish the Tennessee Valley Authority, signed into law on May 18, 1933.

The TVA was a new kind of agency. It was to operate like a private business firm—with the full power of the government behind it. Its job would be "national planning for a complete watershed involving many states and the future lives and welfare of millions."

Taming the river

The TVA construction went ahead with amazing speed. Attacked at a dozen points, the thundering Tennessee River gradually gave in. Massive wedges of concrete were poured into its path. From whirring dam generators a great surge of man-made lightning flashed through the valley.

In time, the TVA was to become the nation's largest single producer of electric power. The dark basin of the Tennessee was lighted up, energized by countless electricity-driven motors and mills, cranes and conveyors, pumps and punch presses. In the city homes of the poor, new appliances began making life more comfortable. Laborsaving devices were appearing on the farms. The TVA's power was cheap enough for all to use. Now the ferocious attack of the utility companies on the government operation could be easily understood. The private companies' rates were more than five times as high as those of the TVA!

The river itself was part of a great life-sustaining cycle. The rain that nurtured the land drained down toward the mainstream. Here every drop of water added its weight to the making of electric power. Nine times the water was re-used as it flowed through each of the TVA power dams, spinning the generators each time. The entire valley tapped the river's power.

Formed by the dams was a chain of lakes, from the mouth of the Tennessee six hundred miles to Knoxville. The rocky rapids of Muscle Shoals were submerged under a placid lake. Water-storage reservoirs kept the channel level high during the dry seasons. For the first time the Tennessee could be navigated year-round by huge barges carrying grain from Omaha, steel from Pittsburgh, oil from the Gulf ports.

Low-cost power produced fertilizer that the poorest farmer could afford. Soon the worn-out land was being renewed, producing high yields.

The TVA threw its weight into an old argument about flood control. For centuries, men had put their full reliance on high mounds of earth. But Senator Norris was no blind believer in levees and dikes. For conditions like those in the Tennessee Valley, he favored what he called nature's way of holding back water, storing it in lakes located in the highlands. Far back from the points where the mountain tributaries joined the main stream of the river, the TVA built a number of flood-control dams at high elevations in the east end of the valley, each forming a reservoir.

It came as a pleasant surprise to the Nebraska senator when the giant new project at Cove Creek was named Norris Dam. When completed, this dam towered 265 feet high. Water was backed up behind a solid concrete barrier, the flow regulated by three gates equal in combined area to a football field.

By the end of 1936 the engineers were ready to give Norris Dam its first tryout. However, nature had a more rigorous test in store.

A sudden thaw brought the melt water gushing down the

mountainsides. A series of swift storms just after Christmas soaked the earth and swelled the feeder streams. In the following weeks the Tennessee River rose steadily. Tension mounted across the valley.

TVA engineers peered at their instruments. Night and day, close watch was kept on the information coming in from scores of volunteer reporting stations throughout the region. A forester, a farmer's wife, a Boy Scout troop, a filling-station operator—each called in the readings on the rain and flow gauges.

The water kept rising in the mainstream. The telegraph message from the TVA control center flashed up into Cove Creek: "Hold everything at Norris Dam!" Torrents continued to fill the river basin. Old-timers in the villages could not remember such a downpour. They recalled the wet seasons that had led to the most destructive floods of the past—but none like this! Nothing now stood between the valley and disaster except Norris Dam, holding a brimming reservoir behind its floodgates.

The rain let up for a few days. But suddenly thunderheads rumbled in from the Gulf. When the new storms let loose, the danger signals were sounded not only in the Tennessee Valley but in the flood-periled towns along the Ohio and the Mississippi. Paducah in Kentucky and Cairo in Illinois were at crisis stage.

Suddenly the rains stopped. In a few days the flood crest was passed. The danger was over. In the long memories of valley people, it remained the frightening winter of 1936–37. But lives and homes and towns were spared. Norris Dam had saved the day!

New environment

The TVA was to become more than electric power or fertilizer, navigation or flood control. Gradually it changed the living environment of an entire region. In planning its programs, the TVA dealt with the valley as a single unit. Within the great seven-state watershed, new patterns began to emerge. Most striking was the change in people's lives.

The drudgery which had made farm men and women old at an early age was lightened by the use of new machinery. People achieved more with their working time and came to enjoy useful leisure. The valley now was healthier. Malaria, which had once struck one out of every four people, began to disappear. The lives of children changed. The food they ate was more nourishing. They were released from endless farm chores to attend school, and the schools of the area were much improved.

But the entire nation remained in the grip of the Depression; although the TVA put thousands to work, widespread unemployment in the Tennessee Valley continued. Few people had achieved comfortable incomes or even a full share of the necessities of life. And yet there was a marked lifting of spirits in place of the old darkness and despair.

Moreover, the improvements did not come as a gift from the gods. The people had a strong sense of being very much a part of the changing conditions. Very early in the TVA experiment, Senator Norris and federal officials realized that the project would be a failure without the full co-operation of the residents of the valley. The program could not be achieved *for* them—only *by* them. Officials discovered that they could not order the personal lives of people as though they were mere symbols on a planning chart.

Experts who came down from Washington with briefcases full of ready-made schemes were in for a rude shock. Nothing seemed to work—until the local people were involved in planning for themselves and had the power to make their own decisions.

The residents put little faith in plans made by those who would not be there to live with the results. TVA officials learned to work through long-standing local organizations, built and trusted by the people. In time the valley dwellers built new organizations through which they could buy and sell more profitably, share the use of heavy equipment, and deal with new community problems as they arose. This was "grass-roots democracy" in action!

Life in the region took a turn for the better, moving with the wheellike patterns in nature. Tree seedlings were planted by the millions to restore barren land. Farmers were taught new methods, using better seeds and fertilizers, rotating crops, and plowing crosswise on the slopes. Families were persuaded to move out of the flood plains to safer ground. Large sections of land were set aside as parks and recreation areas. Conservation became a central feature of TVA planning.

Meanwhile, the Roosevelt administration sponsored conservation programs across the crisis-stricken nation. In the farm lands a vast effort was under way to save the soil from washing and blowing away. Immense public works were initiated for flood control, reforestation, and the building of parks and wildlife areas.

In a highly successful program called the Civilian Conservation Corps, unemployed young men were hired to work on public projects. For millions, many of them city dwellers, this was a useful experience in living in the outdoors, working with nature. They planted two billion trees on denuded and eroded land.

Senator Norris kept close watch on the Tennessee River project. He was well known and well loved in the valley. Townspeople invited him to inspect their new public libraries. Workmen riding the high cranes waved at the familiar white-haired watcher below. And farmers in the back country proudly displayed to him their new milking machines.

The aged Nebraskan had not asked for the leadership of the TVA effort. "I never have known," he said, "how it came to be dumped in my lap." But it fell to him naturally, as though his entire lifetime of struggle had prepared him for this great task. In the closing years of George W. Norris's life his proudest title was "Father of the TVA."

Model communities

As Norris Dam was being built, an attractive, well-planned town was created around it, with curving streets and pleasant open spaces. This town of Norris, Tennessee, was to be the first of a series of model towns designed by the TVA. The latest of these will be Tellico, Tennessee, the TVA's answer to the growing need for new towns in America to ease the pressure on the overcrowded cities in the 1970s.

On fingers of land jutting out into Lake Tellico, this town is being designed as a complete environment for the 25,000 people who will live and work here. In a setting of stunning scenic beauty, Tellico has been planned in advance to cope with its future problems of traffic, waste treatment, and noise control.

The TVA region is a crescent, with one point in the Virginia highlands, swinging down through the heart of the southland, and ending up in the Kentucky bluegrass region. Throughout is a striking series of pictures of the valley's changed life.

Rank after rank of young pines cover the Kentucky hillsides where once the earth was defaced with the spoil banks of strip mines. In outdoor classes, children are taught the meaning of conservation, the need for harmony between man and the natural world around him. In the villages the townspeople meet in their local planning boards. Planning is an ongoing process as the valley continues to struggle with stubborn old problems and an endless series of new ones.

The farmer has learned to work more scientifically. He has spread out his operations into dairying, tree farming, poultry raising—thereby improving his land as well as his income. The region works hard at maintaining clear streams, game reserves, and habitats for wildfowl. As never before, the people are enjoying the outdoors—the man-made mirror lakes, the trout streams, and the pleasure-craft marinas. The beauty of the region has created a new tourist industry.

In the laboratories, TVA scientists are at work on such projects as turning waste matter and garbage into soil conditioners. A constant study is made of the changing patterns of life in the many habitats which are being created here—the reservoirs, the reforested areas, the wildlife reserves.

Clustered about the shore lines are the newest of industries—space rockets, nuclear power, chemicals, electronics, metallurgy. Before it begins operation, every plant is designed with safeguards against pollution of the air and water. By example in its own plants, the TVA lays down the guidelines for private industry, avoiding any damage of the environment. Business firms coming into the area have learned to accept pollution control as a necessary cost of doing business here. The TVA has pioneered in proving that a region can grow in population and in industrial activity—and still have clean streams and pure air.

To all who knew the Tennessee Valley "before and after" the TVA, the truth was as clear as a mountain brook. People and their environment are deeply related to each other. And the health and happiness of this valley depends on moving with the stream of nature, not against it.

Here was a region once caught up in a flood of environmental problems. The answer lay in a program as wide-reaching as the river basin itself and as deep-running as the lives of its people. Because these problems naturally flow together, the solution could be found in a unified approach, as related parts of a whole. The TVA established the river basin or watershed as a workable unit for dealing with the environment.

The conservation movement in the time of Gifford Pinchot and Theodore Roosevelt showed that man must grapple vigorously with environmental crises. The wave of activity led by George W. Norris and Franklin D. Roosevelt profited by old mistakes—but found new answers to new problems.

The TVA proved to be a lasting contribution to man's groping efforts to cope with his surroundings. But to farseeing men it seemed that each age had to inch its way toward its own painful truths. For the dark, rocky journey ahead, there were pathfinders whose lifelong experience had taught them the way.

Well before the present century, Aldo Leopold began to sense the alarming problems of the new age. From the heights above the Mississippi River, he stood watch for signs of trouble. They flared like firebrands against a dark and distant shore.

Aldo Leopold

Lesson of the Land

8. Lesson of the Land

> *All creatures obey the great game laws of nature and fish with nets of such meshes as permit many to escape and preclude the taking of many.*
>
> Samuel Taylor Coleridge

The boy squeezed through the dewy hedge, tossed the morning paper in a long arc onto the porch. In the half-dark he suddenly saw a body stretched out under a clump of pines.

"Aldo," the boy called out in a tense whisper. The reply came back in a throaty grunt, like that of a young bullfrog.

Ed Hunger quietly joined his friend on the wet grass. The two peered into a thicket for a time, listening. Both bodies squirmed forward for a closer look.

Wood ducks! The faint sunglow now clearly showed the female perched at an opening in a hollow tree. The drake hovered nearby, fluttering, twittering, the sunlight sparking color from its jeweled crest.

The boys watched until they had assured themselves that the "woodies" had found a home. To Aldo Leopold and his friend Ed, the nesting of wood ducks was "mighty important." Year by year they had grieved over the steady decline of the wood-duck population in their section of the Mississippi Valley. The small tree-nesting ducks were among the casualties of the changing landscape, the slow disappearance of the forests, the bogs, the wild places.

Burlington, Iowa, was a booming river town in 1887, when both these boys were born. Its life stream was the Mississippi. The current slid slowly past the town's towering headland and its bustling docks, bringing an amazing variety of people and products.

Fine houses stood on the heights. Horses and mules pulled streetcars up the steep bluff, then clambered aboard to coast down in style on the return trip.

In the closing decades of the century, Burlington became an important transfer point where the river trade met the cross-country Chicago, Burlington, and Quincy Railroad. Steamboats hooted and churned at the wharves. But the most spectacular river cargoes of all were the huge timber rafts that floated down the Mississippi from the Wisconsin forests. Thousands of logs were chained together and drifted downstream, guided by a single steamboat.

Year by year, now, Aldo noted that the log rafts coming down the river were fewer in number and smaller in size. In a few years they would be a thing of the dead past, a memory of forests cut to stumps.

Much of Burlington's business was woodworking. Loud was the tumult of its sawmills, busily shaping house lumber and fine furniture, barrels and baskets, carriages and coffins. Burlington's railroad ties crisscrossed the prairie, and its fence posts ran in single file toward every horizon. The town turned out ax handles, plow beams, and gunstocks.

Burlington's dwellings were framed and sided with trimmed lumber. Wagonloads and trainloads of it went out into the treeless plains to become steep-roofed farmhouses and broad-sided barns.

The saws moaned in Aldo's ears. And the sound of them came home to the dinner table where the talk was of the day's events at the family's thriving desk factory.

The Leopolds lived in a stately home high over the river. Aldo's father, a large, sturdy man, enjoyed the outdoors. To his children he transferred his own love of nature and his sense of fairness in dealing with the creatures of the wild community. The Leopolds hunted, but only in moderation. In the spring, when the wildfowl passed through in smaller numbers, bound for breeding and nesting sites, the guns in the household remained in their racks.

Aldo shuddered when he passed Zeller's meat market and saw the slaughtered young geese and ducks hanging out in front. In those days, game was brought in from the nearby marshes by the boatload. And because wildfowl travel and feed and nest in large flocks, they were easy prey for the hunters. To Aldo it seemed that the birds paid a cruel price for their social habits.

Growing up, Aldo Leopold felt a deepening kinship with the wildlife. He changed gradually from a boy simply enjoying the outdoors to a young man caring deeply about what was happening to the natural scene. Some people might be heedless about the living things that shared the earth with them. Others might slash away the virgin forests, slaughter ducks as they brooded their eggs, pour poisons into the streams—and never give it a second thought. But Aldo drew a sharp line between what was good and what was bad for the living landscape on which man made his home.

Reading sign

One blustery morning he was awakened by the flash of fire. Aldo ran to the window and saw a great blaze across the river. He knew its meaning.

A squatter had taken possession of a stretch of marsh along the far shore, which he was trying to turn into a farm. Through his field glasses Aldo had watched the man hacking down the trees, digging ditches, burning great piles of brush.

Aldo knew that slough well. It was a wild tangle of cottonwoods, oozy, matted rushes, and half-drowned islands. Most of all, it was a great nesting area and feeding place for countless transient wildfowl.

To Aldo that wetland appeared to be a foolhardy place to build a homestead. The slough seemed to belong to the river and to the creatures who had previously made it their home. With anger in his heart he had watched the farmer upsetting the patterns in that wild habitat of stilt-legged birds, hut-building muskrats, and giant bullfrogs. Did it make any sense for the farmer to substitute species of his own—cornstalks for cattails and hogs for herons?

The Mississippi Valley is a great flyway of migrating birds. With the river laid out like a clear chart below them, the transients span the continent, northward in the spring and southward in the autumn. Great flocks have followed this ancient route to the timeless rhythm of the seasons. The river valley, with its gentle green hills, was a natural pathway. Along this route the migrants found abundant grain and berries, marsh grasses and pond foods. Season by season, the birds made the same stopovers.

Aldo lived with this busy traffic. Often he watched the slow-beating wings of the big geese aloft, and he could hear the smaller birds passing overhead at night. He learned the habits of the region's migrants and never tired of their comings and goings. Often he prowled alone; sometimes he met his friend Ed, who lived across town. Their common interest was birds. Together they kept lists of the species they spotted. Like a pair of town gossips, they eavesdropped on the new arrivals and chatted over their special finds—the grosbeaks, the rare warblers, the tiny wrens.

Aldo Leopold haunted the dawn. He woke early to spy out the

horned owl, watched it float still-winged and suddenly plummet toward some scurrying prey. Or perhaps curiosity led him on a snow trail of a skunk newly emerged from its winter burrow.

The boy was keen at a game called "reading sign." He could put together from a few clues the story of some brief woodland encounter between predator and prey. He knew that if hunters massacred the foxes in one season, rabbits would overrun the countryside in the next. And if he was selecting a choice spot for fishing, he would sniff the morning air and ask himself: "Now where would I be if I were a smallmouthed bass?"

When he turned sixteen, Aldo began to think about a career. He knew what he would like to do—but did it add up to a job, an income, support for a family of his own? He realized that men placed little value on knowing a raccoon track from that of a 'possum, or on being able to find a secret arbor of wild berries, or on predicting what sort of butterfly would emerge from a certain cocoon.

River's return

That spring the river acted like some great beast which suddenly finds itself caged and shackled. Freeing itself of ice, the current ran swiftly through the March days, its mood dark and threatening. Along its length the river-town people, farmers in the bottom lands, shippers, and boatmen were uneasy.

The valley did not see the sun for nine days of steady rain. From his attic window, Aldo could see the Mississippi rising. The riverbanks were awash. Through his field glasses Aldo watched the squatter on the far side of the river as he piled high a wagon-load of his belongings and vanished.

That morning the two friends crossed the Mississippi in their skiff. Through the mist they could see the remains of the flooded farm. The yellowish water swirled around fresh-cut stumps and piles of fire-scarred brush. A few ridges of earth showed where the homesteader had vainly tried to hold out the river.

As they poled their boat slowly through the foggy slough, the boys expressed their feelings to each other. To Ed, the abandoned farm looked like "an awful lot of wasted work." Aldo could find no sympathy for the man who had mistakenly planned to make this natural bit of wilderness his own. "Served him right," was Aldo's attitude. "This was no place to build a farm."

The river had won this skirmish with one man. But Aldo knew in his heart that the bigger battle was not so easily ended. Men coveted the bottom lands. He had seen places where the sloughs had been drained and diked, shutting out the river . . . and the wildfowl as well.

High overhead a wedge of geese broke ranks. Raucous and trumpeting, they spread, fanned, wheeled, dropped low. The boys could see a few make a landing in a soggy and half-plowed field. The two friends smiled at each other in silence.

They had been brought together by their deep love of nature. They knew also that they would soon be going different ways.

One day soon afterward, Aldo came down to breakfast dressed for travel. He was on his way east to preparatory school.

The elder Leopold spoke that morning of the importance of this step, of the years ahead at college, and of how Aldo would return someday to take over his family's desk factory.

The boy was unusually quiet. Aldo had heard these words before, and he was in no mood to argue with his father on his last morning at home. Someone would have to carry on the business, Aldo understood that very well. But this he also knew: he would not spend his life sitting at desks, or making them.

"*Save the deer!*"

A cold sun poured dawn over the edge of the rimrock. Aldo

Leopold, now a veteran forest ranger, drained his steaming coffee cup, saddled up, and began a day's patrol in the high plateau country of the Southwest.

With his back toward an icy wind, he descended a trailless slope slowly, keeping an eye out for deer. This was a grim fact-finding mission. Across the range the mule deer were spending their worst winter in decades, starving by the thousands.

From the time when he had come into New Mexico and Arizona fresh out of college, Aldo had heard the cry of well-meaning people, "Save the deer!" Many of these were nature lovers, conservationists. To them the deer appeared as timid creatures, defenseless in a savage wilderness. The "villains" were bobcats, wolves, coyotes, and mountain lions. It seemed that the humane thing to do was to save the deer by killing off these predators.

The conservationists were joined in this campaign by the hunters. They not only enjoyed taking the big cats but also received a bounty for every kill. Supporting the crusade were the stockmen, less interested in the deer than they were in preventing the occasional loss of a lamb or a calf to a wild animal.

The total effect of this campaign was slaughter on the range. The large predators were hunted down diligently. Some species were almost exterminated in the Southwest.

But the story had a double twist, unexpected and cruel. Men like Aldo Leopold could have foretold the sad ending. The last act of the tragedy was unfolding now before his eyes.

Once their natural enemies had been eliminated, the deer herds increased at an astounding rate. Overrunning the range in search of food, the "muleys" devoured the browse until it was gone.

As Aldo rode through the valleys, he saw signs of devastation by deer everywhere. Shrubs and twigs and foliage were eaten away as high as the deer could reach. The shoots of low plants were gone, as well as the seedlings of young trees. Aldo had seen

LESSON OF THE LAND 145

what happened when hungry deer invaded croplands, orchards, gardens.

The landscape was as devastated as though stripped by a forest fire or a plague of locusts. In their vastly increased numbers, these animals had become more dangerous than the predators!

Aldo was by now a widely recognized expert in the field of game management. His guiding principle was that the conditions in every natural habitat govern the number of animals that can be supported.

Although animals depend on other living things for food, the natural scene is not like a bloody battleground where species exterminate other species. Instead, all nature is made up of stable, living communities which have a strong grip on survival. Each species produces more offspring every year than can possibly survive. However, their numbers are kept in check partly by their own natural enemies. In the wild, the predators are an essential part of a healthy environment.

In applying the principles of ecology to the region where he was stationed, Aldo studied how animal-population sizes are also limited by such factors as food, shelter, and water. Nature's system of checks and balances maintains the health of the wild community, setting firm limits on population increases. The combination of all these elements fixes what scientists call the carrying capacity of the habitat.

In the plateau country, the deer population had once been in balance with the carrying capacity of the region. And Aldo Leopold was among those who had warned what would happen if men meddled in nature's patterns. In their zeal to do good, conservationists sometimes acted out of a romantic and misguided view of life in the wilds. To them, the predators had seemed cruel—but now these well-intentioned nature groups were themselves responsible for the mass starvation of deer. The muleys had lived here for centuries together with their natural enemies.

But who, Aldo wondered, would protect them from their "friends"?

The morning suddenly turned raw and stormy. Snow turned to sleet, driven by a high wind, as Leopold guided his horse over a stony ridge. Just beyond was a small herd of deer, huddled against the barren hillside, more dead than alive. A few of the bucks still had strength to stand. Some of the does and fawns were far gone toward starvation. As Aldo approached the deer, none of them moved. The forester found them weak, dazed, in a state of shock.

The worst of the winter was still ahead. And Aldo wondered in despair how many thousands of deer were doomed.

Vanishing wilderness

In the 1920s Aldo ranged widely over America's broadest reaches of unspoiled country. But even in the spacious Southwest, he could sense the invasion of man into the last secret strongholds of nature. There were times when he traveled alone across mountain, desert, or plateau, in the pure solitude of a wild landscape—only to run across a billboard, a herd of sheep, a mining claim, a highway. He wondered sometimes whether there was any square foot of America which would not soon be plowed up, rearranged, built over. And if so, how would future generations have any idea what the country had been like in its primitive state?

In those years Aldo began making his plea for something totally new in this nation's experience—pure and protected wilderness. He spoke before organized groups wherever he could, and often he ran into scoffing questions. Of what value was wilderness, and to whom? Were animals more important than men?

The light-haired young forester, azure-eyed and robust, faced his questioners calmly. There was earnest conviction in his strong, bony face. And once people had heard his clear answers, they could hardly doubt the wisdom of his words.

From Leopold came a stream of powerful writings, and his words had a bite to them. He put together the first clear set of ideas about natural habitats and why they must be preserved.

Aldo's search showed that many types of American wilderness were already gone forever—the coastal prairie, the virgin pineries of Wisconsin, the deep hardwood forests of the East Coast, the tall-grass prairie of the Middle West. As for the Far West, Leopold could see the road builder edging into the last remaining unspoiled places, with the parade of motor cars just behind him.

The wild environment is the birthplace of man, he pointed out, urging the preservation of "some tag ends of wilderness" for those who might want to understand something about their own origins. Once any part of it is gone, the world as it once was cannot be restored. The destruction of wild habitats means the end of species that can survive only in a setting unchanged by man. Wilderness is a model of nature from which man has a great deal to learn. Leopold called for the setting aside of areas as huge laboratories where nature could be observed at work.

In 1924 Aldo Leopold secured government approval for America's first wilderness region, a large section at the head of the Gila River in New Mexico. Here man would be an occasional and brief visitor, coming only on horseback, on foot, or by canoe. Forever banned were all roads, timber cutting, or other "improvements." The Gila Wilderness Area became the first of many such regions which would remain the home of wild plants and animals, their communities developing in a natural state amid a primitive environment.

Aldo became one of the founders of the Wilderness Society, an organization dedicated to the safeguarding of natural environments. The protection of wilderness would be an unending battle. And Leopold knew he had fought and won only the first skirmish.

A code for life

Who was this ranger whose defense of nature rang out with such clarity and strength? The University of Wisconsin sought him out and invited him to come to the campus at Madison.

Plan your own courses, Aldo Leopold was told. Teach the lore of wilderness and the science of natural environments. Leopold became the first professor of game management. But he refused to be confined to the classroom.

Aldo now had a large and lively family. He, his wife Estelle, and their five children ranged widely in the "sand counties" around Madison. The children came naturally to a love for the outdoors. It was part of their very growth, their outreach for a set of values and a sense of right and wrong. The Leopold family was nurtured by an appreciation for nature's beauty and a deep relationship with the natural environment.

One spring day in 1930, Aldo came home with the joyous news that he had bought a farm. A real farm? Well, not really—only the ghost of a farm.

The place, just fifty miles north of Madison on the Wisconsin River, was indeed haunted by the spirits of the past. The region still showed the traces of great pine woods, long since logged out. More recent ghosts were those of farmers who had drained the last dregs of fertility from the soil and then abandoned it. A few ruined farm buildings remained. One became "the shack," a shelter in which the Leopolds could stay, coming up from Madison at every opportunity.

Through the wheel of the months, the landscape revealed itself to Aldo Leopold in its many seasonal forms. And he kept a year-round almanac of happenings.

After January's blizzards, Aldo observed that "there is a night of thaw when the tinkle of dripping water is heard in the land." By April he was welcoming *Draba*, "the smallest flower that grows."

One July morning, Leopold arose at 3:30 A.M. and settled himself outdoors with coffeepot and notebook. "Like other great landowners," wrote Aldo, "I have tenants." He went on to record how his "tenants"—field sparrow, robin, indigo bunting, wren—each made its singing claim to territory.

By November, he admitted his admiration for all trees, adding, "But I am in love with pines." In December, the banding of chickadees began an adventure for the family, who would be anxiously hoping five years later that "No. 65290" would return for yet another winter.

Aldo taught his family to cherish the land as though it were a living thing—which indeed it is! He put a spade into the ground, showing his children how even in this exhausted farm land, life still struggled for survival. The region's soil, he explained, was built by the prairie plants, mammals, birds, fungi, insects, bacteria—"all interlocked in one humming community of cooperations and competitions." The living land was the result of thousands of years of living and dying, burning and growing, preying and fleeing, freezing and thawing.

"We abuse land when we regard it as a commodity belonging to us," Leopold later wrote. "When we see land as a community to which we belong, we may begin to use it with love and respect."

Such a view makes each person responsible for whatever he does to the environment, good or bad. It changes man, said Aldo, "from conqueror of the land-community to plain member and citizen of it."

It was not Leopold's style to issue a stern series of "Thou shalt nots." Instead he showed those around him what it meant to live with nature rather than against it. He believed deeply that mankind's moral code should be extended to the total environment if we are to develop a wholesome way of life. This was Leopold's "land ethic," which he was later to set down in a series of brilliant essays, published as *A Sand County Almanac*.

There came a morning when the entire Leopold family stood on a hillside as though waiting for some performance to begin. Aldo put his spade into the ground, twisting it slightly to make an opening. He set in a small pine seedling and, with his heel, tamped the roots into place. He then went on to plant the next young pine, and the next.

Each member of the family caught the rhythm of those few deft movements, and the meaning of them. This was a kind of pine-tree dance, picked up and repeated by each Leopold, including the smallest toddler. In time it became a joyous ritual in which the entire family joined on their outings at the farm. In the spring dusk, figures moved in unison on the land—like the

Winnebago tribesmen who had danced here once in a forested wilderness.

Each year thousands of trees were planted in this fashion. Soon the hillsides were covered with young pines. The Leopold children could feel the land gaining strength and the trees growing taller, as they were themselves. In the autumn evenings, Aldo walked contentedly among the burgeoning pines. He recalled the log rafts of his childhood, the timber shorn from the Wisconsin forests. For one man, the debt to the land was being repaid.

Aldo Leopold taught the ranger's code of leaving behind an environment "at least as good as you found it." Sharing that creed, Rachel Carson was to make living it her life's work.

Rachel Carson

Something in the Wind

9. Something in the Wind

Harm not the earth, neither the sea, nor the trees. . . .
Revelation 7:3

Rachel Carson remembered a town that didn't quite exist. It was a community in mid-America, drowsing in the shade patterns of giant trees, its quiet streets running out toward grainfields and gentle hills.

As she described it, "Even in winter, the roadsides were places of beauty, where countless birds came to feed on the berries and on the seed heads of the dried weeds rising above the snow.

"The countryside was, in fact, famous for the abundance and variety of its bird life, and when the flood of migrants was pouring through in the spring and fall, people traveled from great distances to observe them. Others came to fish the streams which flowed clear and cold out of the hills and contained shady pools where trout lay. . . ."

This was a make-believe land, created in the mind of an imaginative writer. And yet every part of that nonexistent town was well known to Rachel in her growing-up years. In the Pennsylvania of the early decades of this century, scenes of rich beauty appeared to a young girl riding through the countryside in a horse and buggy. Born to be a writer, Rachel set down such sketches in the notebook of her memory. Pieced together out of her own keen observations, these made up her view of an unspoiled America.

There came a spring, however, when something happened to Rachel Carson's imaginary town. "A strange blight crept over the area and everything began to change," she related. "Some evil spell had settled over the community: mysterious maladies swept the flocks of chickens; the cattle and sheep sickened and died. Everywhere was the shadow of death."

In these words, Rachel Carson told her dramatic story of what was really threatening all of this nation. In the year 1962 her book *Silent Spring* appeared. It was the work of an author who had already achieved wide acclaim as a gifted and learned science writer.

From this slight, gentle lady came a book that jarred America. *Silent Spring* fell like a shock wave across this land and around the world. What it said with such clarity and force came out of a long search for the truth about man's relentless struggle against nature. *Silent Spring* was Rachel Carson's disturbing report on a land she loved.

A real world

The western Pennsylvania town in which Rachel Carson was born in 1907 was like a wild flower growing in a wagon rut, gallantly losing its struggle for an older way of life.

Springdale lay stretched out along a sweeping curve of the Allegheny River. The river had become a barge-filled commercial waterway. And the valley was the smoky, clangorous forge of the nation's heavy industry.

Just to the north, oil wells were pumping day and night. Many of the nearby towns were built around mines that pried hard coal from the rocky hills. Furnaces filled the air with smoke and dust as new steelmaking processes poured out glowing rivers of molten metal.

On the Springdale river-front square one morning, three mechanical monsters stood glaring at each other in open rivalry. One was a high-topped horseless surrey that ran slowly and quietly, by electricity. Another was a clumsy giant built around a great boiler—a steam car. The third was a noisy, smelly, sputtering contraption powered by a gasoline engine.

America in those years was making a choice among the three. Or so it seemed from the heated arguments in town squares across this country. But the steel and oil interests were betting heavily on the gasoline-fueled automobile. And that type of motor won out—eventually changing the look, the smell, the sound, and the habits of a nation.

It was a rapidly changing and often confusing time in which Rachel Carson spent her rather sheltered and lonely childhood. The old family farm, acres of tangled woods and fallow fields, was her playground. In the summer days, Rachel and her mother went on outings to the wooded groves on the far edge of the farm. They listened to familiar bird songs. The girl read aloud some of her verses. And the two of them shared homemade delights from a picnic basket. Bright-eyed and pretty, Rachel enjoyed these quiet retreats from the noise and stress of town.

One spring day she made her first trip to Pittsburgh, just eighteen miles away. The city was a smoldering hearth, blackened and dismal. Hills of slag, fuming like volcanoes, encircled the mills. Trains and wagons grubbed ceaselessly around the huge mounds of coal and ore. Fires from thousands of furnaces, smelters, and foundries flared in the gloom. Smoke and soot drifted up from what seemed like a bottomless pit.

The shy, sensitive Rachel was repelled at first glance by the city. But she had taught herself to look soberly at things as they are. All this too was part of the reality of life. Her thought was to take written form in later years: "If the world is to be understood at all, it has to be understood as a whole—open-hearth furnaces and orioles, April sun and adding machines."

At college in Pittsburgh, Rachel became deeply interested in science. But she could see with dismay that many of the science-minded young people of the town were being drawn into the laboratories of the mills and factories. Not only was industry taking over vast areas of America's landscape and resources; the minds of educated men and women were being turned toward products and processes, markets and profits.

Writing and nature were the double wheels around which Rachel's life turned. And these interests moved her purposefully toward her career.

Wheels of life

As a sailor sometimes yearns for port, so many an inlander dreams of the sea. Having grown up in a landlocked, mountain-ringed valley, Rachel Carson was drawn toward the ocean by some nameless, deep-felt urge. In her days of postgraduate study, she reached the seacoast at last—and never really left it again.

The sea welcomed her. It became her habitat for a lifetime. Like a shore bird, she ranged the moss-covered rocks and the sandy beaches, exploring the rich variety of life. She clambered aboard scientific vessels, and for weeks at a time she sailed with a fishing fleet, peering into the dark waters, eagerly checking whatever came up in the nets. Roaming the ocean front from Newfoundland to the Florida Keys, she was a watcher at the tide pools and salt marshes, putting together the total picture of rock, air, water, plants, animals—and man.

In these years she was biologist and teacher, editor and writer. In 1941 came the first of her series of sea books. Each was a work of science and a work of art.

All of nature throbs with the rhythm of a great set of turning wheels. And Rachel Carson became absorbed in the workings of these interlocking cycles of change.

Life-giving water circulates in various forms and states—as rising vapor and clouds, rain and snow, clinging droplets of moisture, flowing streams and seas.

Oxygen, essential to life, combines with other chemicals to circulate through plants and animals. Other elements—nitrogen, carbon, hydrogen—each make orderly rounds through the ever-changing environments of the earth.

Green plants are the first step in a round-robin transfer of the energy which they derive from the light of the sun. Plants are eaten by animals, which in turn are eaten by meat eaters, relaying the sun-born energy around the wheel of life.

The food chains of the sea begin with the tiny plant plankton, which are eaten by animal plankton. These make up the food of small fish, which are the food-energy sources for large fish. One of the greatest of life's wheels has its hub in the sea, where life itself once began. And Rachel Carson studied closely the complex patterns of what she called "the cycles of use and return."

Each of these wheels, the writer-scientist observed, is fragile, delicately balanced in its motion, easily upset. Rachel Carson could see where some unknown disturbances had turned the ocean-shore rocks white with a heavy overgrowth of barnacles or had suddenly given rise to an immense school of jellyfish, floating offshore in miles of ghostly, pulsing forms. Even a temporary breakdown of the harmony among species might throw the workings of nature out of order.

Man, too, is a part of the life-sustaining cycles in nature. Involved in their workings just as surely as is any other species, he depends for survival on their orderly movement.

Modern man has learned how to send the big wheels spinning in new directions. He has rearranged food chains and altered the chemistry of the soil, the air, the water. In the breeding of livestock and pets, flowers and grains, he has intervened in nature's patterns. He has achieved the power to alter the living landscape, changing temperatures and moisture movements. There were even species of plants and animals which became extinct through man's actions.

Could man unwittingly jam the wheels of nature, bringing them to a standstill?

Environment zero

To Rachel Carson, the answer soon came with shattering force. On August 6, 1945, an atomic bomb was exploded over Hiroshima, Japan. The next years of building and testing ever larger nuclear weapons proved that man had achieved a heart-chilling power to destroy life.

Each charred, barren bomb-test site proved to be something quite rare on this earth, a place where nothing could live—Environment Zero!

For a life scientist like Rachel Carson, this period was full of anguish. "I clearly remember," she later recalled, "that in the days before Hiroshima I used to wonder whether nature actually needed protection from man.

"Surely the sea was inviolate and forever beyond man's power to change it. Surely the vast cycles by which water is drawn up by the clouds to return again to the earth could never be touched. And just as surely the vast tides of life—the migrating birds—would continue to ebb and flow over the continents, marking the passage of the seasons. But I was wrong." A new age had begun, full of peril for the fragile, wheeled vehicle on which life moves.

Rachel Carson, meanwhile, focused her attention on still another kind of danger. A letter from a friend prompted her to deepen her study of a sinister new scourge—something in the wind, in the soil, in the food, in the water.

Spray of death

Through four and a half years of patient research, Rachel Carson intensively probed the use of pesticides in America.

These powerful chemical killers were developed to fight off various kinds of organisms which are considered dangerous to crops. Over a period of many years such poisons were being more widely used, the quantities being steadily increased, the methods becoming more reckless. By the late 1950s a massive assault was being carried on by means of sprayers from tank trucks, tractors, and airplanes. Some agricultural communities were saturated with such pesticides as DDT.

This was a time when agricultural production in the United States was increasing rapidly. It is now known that the main factors in higher farm productivity were improved seed, wiser crop planning, better fertilizers. However, the chemical industry claimed that modern farming methods had come to depend heavily on the widespread use of chemical agents.

Ecologists and others recognized that no such large-scale chemical warfare on the land was possible without serious side effects. Rachel Carson was appalled at just how much damage was being done. As she soon learned, the main victims of the pesticides were not the pests, nor were weeds the only victims of herbicides.

In many laboratories her fellow scientists were at work getting at the truth about the new poisons. Rachel Carson saw why the pesticides had little effect in dealing with the insects against which they were aimed. These insect populations were largely controlled in numbers by their natural enemies. This is nature's way of keeping species in balance with each other. However, the pesticides killed off the natural enemies of the pests just as effectively as they killed the bothersome insects.

As new insect generations were produced in rapid succession, some hardy mutant individuals appeared which had an inborn resistance to the pesticides. These formed the basis for new breeds upon which the poisons had little or no effect. Soon the farmers were using even deadlier sprays, in larger quantities.

The new substances were by-products of a search for chemical agents to be used in war. Insects were used in the laboratory testing. It was in this way that chemists found they had made a series of powerful killers. Soon sprayers were scattering these poisons to the four winds.

Instead of singling out a specific target, the pesticides attacked a wide range of living things. Widespread evidence had been gathered to show that the poisons entered deeply into the food cycles by which all of nature lives. As Rachel Carson pointed out, the careless use of the spray doomed "the pets of the family, the farmer's cattle, the rabbit in the field, the lark out of the sky."

Because these chemical compounds are synthetic, they act in an unexpected way. For example, DDT is not readily eliminated as waste matter by certain species, such as birds. Instead it remains in the tissues, gradually building up in volume as more of it is taken in.

Fellow scientists showed Rachel Carson traces of DDT in the bodies of birds and fish, frogs and small mammals. Every watershed in America was washing this substance from the land into the running streams and seas. Gradually DDT was being transferred to every part of the planet, even showing up in penguins in the Antarctic and in Arctic lemmings.

Most sinister of all was the fact that these poisons are relayed in deadly doses from parents to offspring. An elm tree is sprayed with the pesticide, and its leaves fall to the ground. The leaves are eaten by worms which themselves may not be killed. But the robin which eats the worms may die of the poison—or pass it on to its young.

Rachel Carson saw "a rain of poison falling from the skies into the world of wildlife." As she wrote the opening chapter of her book, she pictured the fictional town of an America that used to be . . . and the strange stillness that came one spring when the birds lay dead. "On the mornings that had once throbbed with the dawn chorus of robins, catbirds, doves, jays, wrens, and scores of other bird voices there was no sound; only silence lay over the fields and woods and marsh."

In rising anger, Miss Carson demanded to know "who has the right to decide" about the use of these mass killers? Who has been given the power of life and death over the wildlife?

With the caution of a responsible scientist, Rachel Carson could only set down what was known at the time about the possible effects of the pesticides on man. However, research had already begun to show evidences of the build-up of DDT in the human body. And pesticides had definitely produced cancer in mice and other mammals. It was possible that these chemical agents could have a dangerous effect on man.

In *Silent Spring* the alarming facts were presented in detail. Courageously she brought to public attention the large body of truth discovered by science. Rachel Carson, a dedicated scientist, had written her story. A modest and gracious lady had dared to take on the powerful chemical industry!

Giant corporations tried without success to discredit Rachel Carson's conclusions. They charged that the book exaggerated the dangers, that she had gone too far. Miss Carson only wondered fearfully whether she had gone far enough.

"It is we"

Man had indeed blundered mindlessly into the delicate inner workings of life.

And with no time to spare, Rachel Carson helped make the world aware that even the most innocent-appearing changes in the environment must be looked at with suspicion. Though with good intentions, men were moving into realms they did not fully understand.

New chemical substances were being put carelessly to a variety of uses faster than they could be properly tested and their effects studied. Many of these substances produced no visible signs of disease or damage. Often they were even without taste, smell, or color. Human beings seemed able to adjust to these chemical changes in the environment. Their effects might be delayed for years. The long-range results were unknown.

Man-made substances, like strontium-90, dropped from the skies in radioactive fallout after nuclear-bomb testing—and were taken in by cows eating grass, transferred to human beings in milk, even passed on to children in their own mothers' milk!

Clearly a new series of hazards to life on earth had appeared. There was now more than one way that man could destroy himself, along with the rest of living nature.

The 1960s saw a deepening concern, too, over a world's growing population. Were there enough resources on the planet for all, enough food, oxygen, space? Rising population was linked with new advances in medical science and other developments which lengthened the human life span.

Even though more children survived than ever before, large families continued to be the pattern in many parts of the world, often based on age-old custom and belief. Population increased in many of the newly independent countries, though they were still gripped by the poverty and ignorance in which they had been left by centuries of colonial bondage.

However, some experts felt that the worst population problems were in America, declaring that the arithmetic of human numbers does not tell the whole story. This was a country, they pointed out, in which people consume much more than their share of the world's resources. Americans were voracious users of power and were thoroughly polluting this country through the production and use of that power.

It was estimated that every American used power equal to the energy of five hundred slaves. Multiply that by the country's 200 million persons, the experts said, if you want to see the real depth of America's population—and pollution—problems!

To Rachel Carson, a possible deathblow for all mankind seemed a real threat from many directions. And her last years were spent not only trying to protect nature from man, but also defending man from his own acts.

"His war against nature is inevitably a war against himself," she warned. "His heedless and destructive acts enter into the vast cycles of the earth and in time return to him."

Speaking on a college campus in 1962, the writer-scientist recounted the new hazards to life. "Today we use the sea as a dumping ground for radioactive wastes, which then enter into the vast and uncontrollable movements of ocean waters through the deep basins, to turn up no one knows where," she declared.

"The once-beneficent rains are now an instrument to bring down from the atmosphere the deadly products of nuclear explosions. Water, perhaps our most precious natural resource, is being misused at a reckless rate. Our streams are fouled with an incredible assortment of wastes—domestic, chemical, radioactive.

"We now wage war on other organisms, turning against them all the terrible armaments of modern chemistry, and we assume the right to push whole species over the brink of extinction."

Before an audience of students, she told of her hopes that her fellow scientists, the men and women of her own generation, might have carried out their responsibilities to America's tomorrow. "Alas, this cannot be said," Miss Carson admitted with deep feeling, "for *it is we* who have brought into being a fateful and destructive power."

Rachel Carson did not live to see that her *Silent Spring* signaled a rising new reply to humanity's perils. Following the publication of this book came the first moderate but serious response to the environmental crisis.

The international test-ban treaty was signed, curbing bomb testing in the atmosphere and outlawing radioactive fallout. By law, the use of DDT and other dangerous chemicals was restricted. A series of threats to natural conservation sites such as the Grand Canyon, the California redwoods, and the Florida Everglades were effectively opposed. The Wilderness Act was passed by Congress, safeguarding vast nature areas for the future.

But this whole nation was not yet ready for a new decision. A major part of the American economy remained tied up in products and processes that damage the environment: internal-combustion engines; farming with the use of dangerous poisons; plastic and metal containers that seem to have everlasting existence; industrial methods that befoul the air, water, and land.

The cities of America had given over their clean water and pure air to private business as a free gift, worth literally billions of dollars a year. Many public agencies were themselves guilty of ecological crimes. Even more disturbing was the continued unwillingness of people to change fixed styles of living—patterns that have led us to the edge of environmental disaster.

Less than ten years after the publication of *Silent Spring*, the cry of a magnificent bird was silenced at last. The peregrine falcon vanished from its cliffside habitats, the first species ever killed off by chemicals. DDT had destroyed its ability to lay normal eggs.

Thoreau's Walden lay surrounded by a fast-growing urban complex that stretched from Boston to Washington, D.C.—congested and sprawling, planless and ugly.

Portions of Olmsted's Central Park were narrowly saved from invading bulldozers only by repeated citizens' protests.

Not a session of Congress passed without new attempts to raid the national forests that Pinchot once safeguarded.

And Muir's beloved Sierra was not allowed a moment's peace by the dam builders, resort promoters, wildlife destroyers.

America had heard the warnings from its devoted guardians of the environment. And yet the nation hoped to postpone a reckoning. Still ahead was a time of trial, a moment for choice.

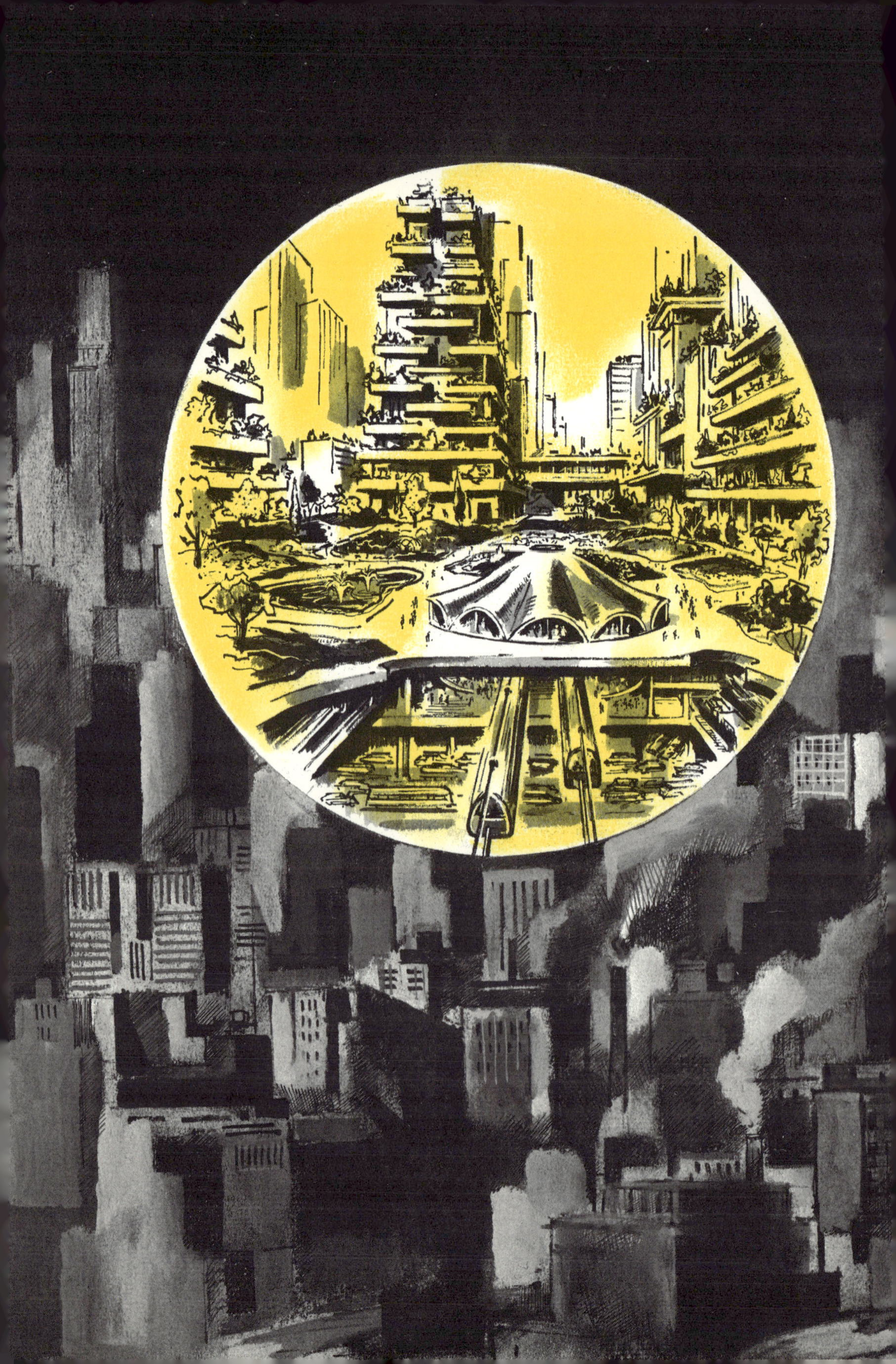

Man the Choice Maker

10. Man the Choice Maker

*Accuse not Nature, she hath done her part;
Do thou but thine.*

                              John Milton

The American is sometimes pictured as a person whose needs come down to very few—in fact, only one. All he wants is—"More!"

If this is true, the American succeeded beyond his most wishful dreams. He gained abundance—and enough to spare. In two hundred years this nation moved steadily toward what has been called "a high standard of living."

If the measuring rod is in tons of food, numbers of automobiles, and quantities of services, home furnishings, clothing, playthings, appliances—then the standard is indeed high.

In recent years, however, many people began using a different yardstick. They looked closely at this country's life-style and asked new kinds of questions. They wanted to know about America not as a machine for grinding out goods but as a setting for the fullest possible enjoyment of life. Important to them was not so much the material riches of their nation but an enriched pattern of living. Instead of asking "How much, how many?" they wanted to know "How good?"

From questions of this sort came some new ways of thinking about America's true standard of living. Clearly, no quantity of air conditioners can substitute for air that is naturally pure. Motorboats and sailboats in endless numbers lose their attractiveness when the lakes and bays are full of filth. The more automobiles there are, the more they defeat themselves, tied up in traffic jams. America had become a great consumer of commodities, but the country was slowly being smothered in the resulting pollution.

Gradually it was becoming clear that the quantities of goods and the quality of the environment were often in conflict with each other. Strangely enough, more products could sometimes mean a *lower* standard of living! Suddenly aware of his environment, the American took another look at himself and his way of life.

This American is known world-wide for the excellence of his bathroom plumbing—hooked up, however, to inadequate sewage systems. His auto trips to the nearby shopping center are powered by a hundred horses or more—and the exhaust fumes fill the air. He has packaged his fruits and vegetables in sanitary containers—often with DDT inside the package. He has filled the average home with scores of plugged-in appliances—leaving a trail of pollution from the factories where they are made and the electricity plants that produce the power, to the junk piles where they eventually wind up.

Bewildering! "The more we have," ran a common complaint, "the less we seem to be enjoying it." The time seemed to have run out for evading some hard decisions. A greater quantity of goods—or a higher quality of life? Was it necessary to lower the material "standard of living"—or could the search continue for ever higher standards, based, however, on a more realistic understanding of human needs?

In the 1960s our attention was fixed on the moon, and we reached it. In the 1970s we would redirect our hopes toward the earth, man's home.

Creature of Earth

In the busy streets of any city, it is possible to believe we are in a completely artificial, man-made environment. But with all his knowledge and inventiveness, man has found no substitutes for the natural things which sustain his life.

Even in man's most arrogant, high-flown moments, nature has a way of bringing him back to earth. Just at the time when he is feeling most independent comes the jarring reminder that he had better pay closer attention to the world around him. Nature's warning is carried in the wind and thundered from the skies.

It may come as a snowstorm or as an electrical blackout that leaves a giant city powerless and paralyzed. Smog may fill the hospitals with gasping patients. A drought can make an entire region dust-dry, especially where pollution has already caused a shortage of pure water. A blight across the land may destroy essential foods.

And yet, when nature is kind and bountiful, the earth seems so perfectly fitted to man's needs. The truth, of course, is that man evolved to suit the planet.

Developing through countless previous forms, his species appeared in the last great ice age as one of the new mammals of the era. Since then, and for all time, he is interlocked with the earth and the creatures that live on it. The natural world is the home of man. It surrounds him, enters his being. His very survival depends on its condition.

When he endangers those with whom he shares the planet, he too is in danger. If he makes the earth unlivable, there is no other place he can go. Anywhere else he is a fish out of water, a bird locked in the cage of whatever temporary, artificial home he might devise. He can never completely escape from his own natural environment. It is forever as close to him as his next sip of water, morsel of food, breath of air.

Not bound by man's fixed borders, the natural world is one world. The earth's residents share the struggle for life as they share the sun. There is no place to hide from air- and waterborne pollution that spreads from one region to the next. Each country foretells future problems to its neighbor. From the so-called advanced countries come dire warnings to those which hasten to catch up.

Japan has begun the use of vending machines that dispense a whiff of oxygen. From the Netherlands comes word that the butterflies have all but disappeared, victims of pesticides. Clouds carrying radioactive substances move ominously across the skies. The seas, available to all, give up poison-bearing fish.

If this earth is in truth man's only home, how can he live in it at peace with nature? How can he achieve a truly higher "standard of living" on this planet? What choices are still in his hands?

Some answers are now coming from those who are the Thoreaus, Olmsteds, Leopolds, of today. Other clues are to be found in the environment itself—the place where each of us will live out the rest of his life.

Who chooses?

An industrialist, once visiting a quiet and beautiful valley, remarked that he planned to improve it. "But how?" his hosts wanted to know. "I'm going to dot it with factories," he replied.

Not so long ago, townsfolk readily welcomed such proposals. But in time, communities became wary. Once the local people only wanted to know about a new plant, "How many will it employ?" and "How much will it produce?" Now it is likely that the builders will be asked, "What happens to the environment?"

In the past, the disrupting of nature's pattern was looked upon as a matter of necessity. Now it is seen as a matter of choice.

Men cannot leave the land untouched. They are numerous residents of the earth and need to use the resources of the planet in order to survive. But they have a wide range of life-styles from which to select. And the use of supersonic jet planes, the building of a huge dam, the pumping of offshore oil—these are decisions to be made carefully.

Who makes the choices? Public officials, business leaders, engineers, scientists? Too often this country has been led into errors, some of which can never be undone. The American landscape is strewn with the wreckage of unwise ventures.

How did these misfortunes occur? Did they result from ignorance or from greed? Some seem to have been the blunders of a society groping for what it thought was the good life. Others came about because the warnings of watchful people and omens on the landscape were ignored. Back in the early days of this nation, men polluted their environment without knowing what they were doing. But today there is hardly any excuse for heedless damage.

The ecologist is able to trace out long-range and far-reaching consequences. What will result from draining a swamp, using a new pesticide, tampering with the weather, building a new power plant? These are matters that concern the ecologist. His business is to track down the chains of causes and effects, the weblike interrelations among living things. When all the facts are brought together, then a more reasonable judgment is possible.

With America's technology moving rapidly and on a large scale into new ventures, the hidden hazards are many. There seems to be a need for what has been called an "early warning system" to alert the nation when environmental dangers appear. Scientists are being urged to serve in watchtowers over this land.

However, science holds no magic powers. It is not a shrine where men pray for nature's blessings. Science is a way of organizing man's knowledge about himself and the world around him. And scientific information can lead to the making of better choices.

As for the engineer or technician, the inventor of our technology, he cannot be held to blame for our problems. His help is needed now more than ever. Our society cannot abandon its technical knowledge nor return to a primitive way of life. Today's engineer can be presented with the modern problem: how can a better environment become the chief product of today's technology?

There is no sure way of avoiding error. But in a free society, the best hope seems to lie in the people themselves, people who are informed and involved. America's millions have discovered that whatever hurts the total environment affects their well-being. And the mood of today is to question everything which might possibly change desirable patterns of life in any significant way.

Painfully, the people have learned that they themselves must become the guardians of the nation's future. Their vigilance appears to be the only defense against private interests' claiming a right to plunder, to pollute, to destroy. An active and aroused public is the only safeguard against the despoiling of the land.

Perhaps the most difficult choices are those to be made within each family circle—or in each person's search for a better way to live.

Hope for tomorrow

In the 1970s a handful of guardians of America's environment suddenly became multitudes. Thin, single voices crying out for caution were joined by a rising, rumbling chorus.

In the very forefront of the new movement came the young

people. With a surging enthusiasm they carried banners emblazoned with an "E"—for Earth, Ecology, Environment.

Somehow they had heard the warnings of Marsh and Rachel Carson. They knew Thoreau's words by heart. Their hopes and values were close to those of Olmsted and Muir. They made it clear that they would not tolerate a ruined earth. And the land began to ring with youthful demands for change.

It seemed that at a given moment, the nation's patience with pollution, its apathy at a worsening world, broke down. A wave of anger and zeal was touched off by still one more puff of poison into the atmosphere, another ooze of green acid into the river. A deep concern for America's condition reached into every corner of the land, voiced by people of all ages and sorts.

The sounds of protest were heard in Washington and in the board rooms of big corporations. Environment became a top issue in local and national politics. Organizations that had been stubbornly fighting the conservation battles for decades found added strength and vigor. New groups sprang up everywhere—sometimes concentrating on a single local problem, or else focused on the big picture of the degraded landscape. Some groups shouted, "Action now!" Others pleaded for long-range and deep-running changes in America's policies and its social values.

Again and again was heard the cry for action that would end the downhill trend and restore health and wholesomeness to the American scene. Some of the main ideas came straight out of Thoreau and Marsh. Others were as new as the latest insights of science.

In Menlo Park, California, a private company operating with government backing built a plant which turns tons of trash into thousands of kilowatts of electrical power. The plant is small and experimental, a model of what can be done.

In northern Wisconsin, polluted Snake Lake has been drained bone-dry. The water was pumped 1500 feet uphill and released. The hope is that the lake will again fill up, the water filtered and purified by its return trip underground.

In Chicago, a corporation owned by black people gathers and bales old newspapers which have been brought by citizens to collection stations throughout the city and suburbs. Instead of being burned, the waste paper is used to make new newsprint. Recycled in this way, each ton of paper saves seventeen trees.

San Francisco, Baltimore, and New Orleans are all examples of cities in which the people have rejected expressways going into the inner city, choosing instead to develop speedy, efficient, pollution-free mass transportation systems.

Rebellions have been staged against the "convenience" of nonreturnable bottles—which actually do return in the form of a trash problem which has no solution. As one ecologist put it: "There is no longer an 'away' where we can throw things." Scores of towns have banned the sale of the throwaway bottle.

Many river-edge towns have begun to grapple with the problem of reducing water pollution to the point where the rivers can begin to cleanse and renew themselves.

University campuses, where the wide range of gathered knowledge matches the diversity of nature itself, have become centers of planning and action on the environmental problems of the surrounding regions. At Yale the effort is concentrated in the School of Forestry, founded in 1900 by Gifford Pinchot.

The problem of the motor car is being challenged vigorously at its source—the automobile industry, which has yet to design a car suited to our safety needs.

Stricter laws have been passed at every level of government—setting quality standards for the environment, forbidding certain harmful practices, setting up taxes and penalties for the abuse of water and air.

Across this land, a repeated series of demands has set practical goals for today and tomorrow.

> Smoke, junk, sewage—all represent matter which in some form came out of the earth. Restore it once again to the cycles of nature and life.
>
> Plan life in the cities so that people will not flee from them at every chance.
>
> It is not enough to have clean air and water in the remote places of the continent. These must become part of where most of America lives—in and around the large centers of population.
>
> Some of the worst American environments are the result of poverty—the black ghettoes of the large cities, the hunger-racked hills of Appalachia, the reservations where Indian families barely survive; these must be eliminated by our affluent society.
>
> There is no right to pollute, no freedom to poison the air which must be used by all, no permission to contaminate the public waterways and water supplies.
>
> It may be costly, but some line can be drawn beyond which the bulldozers cannot go, where there is open space and greenery, where the last wild marshes will not be filled and the wooded hillsides left intact.
>
> We can't give back life to the passenger pigeon. Nor can we bring back the tons of topsoil that the rivers have carried to the sea. But we can save hundreds of species now in danger of extinction. And vast wild areas can still be preserved—for no purpose at all except their intrinsic value as part of living nature.

These are some of the goals of a movement which cannot settle for any half measures. Its supporters seem to be in no mood for piecemeal efforts or for putting a pretty face on pollution, for hiding danger behind a screen or for avoiding solutions by making promises. The truths about America's threatened environment have become self-evident. Life and liberty are once again at stake in this country—as well as the pursuit of happiness.

After two centuries, America's people are moving in the 1970s to their most vigorous defense yet of the land in which they live. The choices they face are challenges as urgent as those that confronted the founders of the nation.

Perhaps the clearest symbol of the new day appeared in Congress. An amendment was proposed to the Constitution, written in the spirit of Thomas Jefferson.

"Every person has the inalienable right to a decent environment," the amendment declared. "The United States and every state shall guarantee this right."

Suggestions for Further Reading

Carson, Rachel. *Silent Spring.* Houghton Mifflin, 1962. This is the book that stirred America to the danger of the chemical destruction of our environment.

Commoner, Barry. *Science and Survival.* Viking, 1966. Choices still left to mankind are outlined in this sober report on our endangered world.

Dasmann, Raymond F. *The Last Horizon.* Macmillan, 1963. "There's not much room left," writes a noted ecologist, telling of the world-wide battle to save some unspoiled areas.

Frome, Michael. *Whose Woods These Are.* Doubleday, 1962. As rich background to the conservation story of Gifford Pinchot, this book tells of the national forests and their importance to all of us.

Hirsch, S. Carl. *The Living Community: A Venture into Ecology.* Viking, 1966. In the companion to *Guardians of Tomorrow,* the author explains the patterns of interdependence in nature.

Leopold, Aldo. *A Sand County Almanac.* Oxford University Press, 1966. A naturalist tells with great strength and tenderness his beliefs about the land and its meanings for mankind.

Marsh, George Perkins. *Man and Nature* (David Lowenthal, editor). Belknap Press, 1965. More than a hundred years old, this remarkable work is still one of the best explanations of man's unwitting harmfulness in dealing with nature.

Norris, George W. *Fighting Liberal.* Macmillan, 1945. The former senator from Nebraska tells his own story of a life devoted to the needs of man in a changing American environment.

Shepard, Paul, and McKinley, Daniel, editors. *The Subversive Science: Essays Toward an Ecology of Man.* Houghton Mifflin, 1968. A wide-ranging anthology of articles by authorities who view an understanding of ecology as essential to man's future.

Swift, Hildegarde Hoyt. *From the Eagle's Wing.* Morrow, 1962. This biography traces the adventures of John Muir from a Wisconsin farm to the Western mountains, a story told with deep understanding and imagination.

Teale, Edwin Way, editor. *The Wilderness World of John Muir.* Houghton Mifflin, 1954. A famous American naturalist has put together some of the best writings of John Muir, along with his own pointed comments.

Udall, Stewart L. *The Quiet Crisis.* Holt, Rinehart, & Winston, 1963. Here is the story of a courageous battle against the plunder of America's resources.

Index

Advertising industry, 119
Agriculture, Department of, 102, 106, 107
Air pollution, 20, 70, 119
Alabama, 88
Allegheny River, 155
American Company, explosion at powder mill of, 34–35
American Revolution, 24
Appalachian Mountains, 120
Arizona, 144
Atomic bomb, 159
Automobile industry, problems in, 176

Balance of nature, 49, 145
Baltimore, 175
Baseball, 67
Berea, Ohio, 115
Birds, Leopold's interest in, 140, 141, 142, 149
Blue Ridge Mountains, 120
Bobcats, hunting of, 144
Boll weevil, 89
Boone, Daniel, 124

Bottles, nonreturnable, ban of, 175
Broken Bow, Nebraska, 125
Buffalo herds, 77, 85
Burlington, Iowa, 139
Burlington, Vermont, 43, 44
Burroughs, John, quoted, 24
Butterflies, destroyed by pesticides, 171

Cairo, Illinois, 130
California, 67, 85, 165
Canada, 81
Carbon, 158
Carrying capacity of habitat, 145
Carson, Rachel, 151, 154–62, 164, 174; ocean studied by, 157, 158; on pesticides, 160, 161–62; in Pittsburgh, 156–57; quoted, 154, 155, 159, 164; sea books by, 157; *Silent Spring* by, 155, 162, 164, 165
Census Bureau, U.S., 89

Central Park, in New York City, 62–67, 68, 165
Chattanooga, Tennessee, 121
Chicago, 61; Columbian Exposition in, 88; "Riverside" as suburb of, 70; waste paper recycled in, 175
China, Olmsted's trip to, 58
Cigarette smoking, 119
"City beautiful" movement, 68
Civil War, 50, 67, 81, 104, 114
Civilian Conservation Corps, 132
Coleridge, Samuel Taylor, quoted, 138
Columbian Exposition, 88
Columbus, Christopher, 88
Communities in nature, 96, 145, 150
Community: model, 132; planning of, 69–70
Concord, Massachusetts, 21, 24–29 *passim*, 34
Connecticut, 57
Conservation, 133, 134, 174; as battle cry, 110; as feature of TVA, 132; *see also* Ecology; Environment; Nature
Constitution, U.S., and proposed amendment for better environment, 177.
Continental Congress, Second, 14, 15

Coolidge, Calvin, 123
Coyotes, hunting of, 144
Crockett, Davy, 124

Darwin, Charles, 46
DDT, 160, 161, 169; build-up of, in living tissue, 161, 162; legal restriction in use of, 165; peregrine falcon destroyed by, 165
Deer, 77, 144, 145, 146
Depression, Great, 131
Detroit, 125
Douglas fir, 86
Draba, 149
Drought, 170
Ducktown, Tennessee, 121–22
Dust storms, 125

Eastern seaboard, and West, 104
Ecology, 50, 145, 160, 172, 174; *see also* Conservation; Environment; Nature
Edison, Thomas, 89
Electric power, 120, 129, 130
Electronics, 134
Elk Hills, California, 118
Environment: organizations for protection of, 174–75; pollution of, 20, 41, 47, 48, 70, 89, 119, 164, 169–77 *passim*; scientific resources for saving,

49, 173; *see also* Conservation; Ecology; Nature
Everglades, Florida, 165

Factory system, evils of, 33
Falcon, peregrine, destroyed by DDT, 165
Fall, Albert B., 118
Fallout, radioactive, 163, 164
Famine, as result of land abuse, 48
Fertilizer, 129, 130, 160; nitrates in, 117
Fir, Douglas, 86
Fire protection, 71
Flood, 114, 121; as result of land abuse, 48
Flood control, 129, 130
Florida, 119, 165
Food chains, 158; of sea, 158
Ford, Henry, 118
Forest fires, 104
Forestry, 94, 99, 100, 101, 103, 104, 106, 107, 108, 109, 110; School of, at Yale, 176
Forests: as clustering of communities, 96; destruction of, 96–97; national, 98; reserved, 97, 98, 107; *see also* Lumber industry

Game management, 145, 148
Gila River, 148
Gila Wilderness Area, 148
Grand Canyon, 101, 165
Grazing animals, 77, 105
Great Lakes, 97
Great Smoky Mountains, 120
Green plants, 158
Gulf states, 97

Habitat, carrying capacity of, 145
Harding, Warren G., 118
Harrison, Benjamin, 97
Herbicides, 160
Hiroshima, bombing of, 159
Homestead Act, 81
Hookworm, 124
Hoover, Herbert, 123, 125
Hunger, Ed, 138, 141, 143
Hyde Park, New York, 127
Hydrogen, 158

Indianapolis, 83
Indians, American, 96, 104, 116, 151
Insects, resistant to pesticides, 160–61
Interior, Department of, 106, 118

Jefferson, Thomas, 14, 15, 16–17, 19, 20, 177; as President, 17–18

Kentucky, 133
Knoxville, Tennessee, 121, 129

Land, abuse of, 48, 49, 77, 89, 122, 127, 150
Leopold, Aldo, 135, 138–51; as forest ranger, 144; as game-management expert, 145, 148; land ethic of, 150; pines grown by, 150–51; *Sand County Almanac* by, 150; at University of Wisconsin, 148; and wildlife, kinship with, 140, 141, 149
Life, quality of, 168–70, 171
Lincoln, Abraham, 45, 81
Livestock, grazing of, 77, 105
Lumber industry, 95, 97, 98, 99, 103, 107; *see also* Forests

McKinley, William, 105
Madison, Wisconsin, 148, 149
Malaria, 124, 131
Man and Nature (Marsh), 48, 50
Marsh, George Perkins, 35, 38–40, 41, 42–51, 174, 175; as Congressman, 44–45; as diplomat, 45, 47; as fish commissioner, 46–47; *Man and Nature* by, 48, 50; as scholar, 43
Massachusetts, industrialization of, 32

Menlo Park, California, 175
Middle West, 78, 97, 147
Milk, strontium-90 in, 163
Milton, John, quoted, 168
Mississippi River, 121, 130, 135, 139, 141, 142–43
Model communities, 133
Mountain lions, hunting of, 144
Mountains of California, The (Muir), 87
Muir, Daniel, 74, 75, 76, 78, 79
Muir, John, 71, 74–87, 90–91, 165, 174; boyhood of, 74–80; education of, 79–80; inventions of, 79–80, 82; journal of, 84, 85; *Mountains of California* by, 87; as naturalist, 86–87; and Pinchot, 101; and Sierra Club, 90; Western highlands described by, 90
Muscle Shoals, 116–20 *passim*, 122, 123, 126, 127, 129

Nation, The, Olmsted as editor of, 67
Nature: balance of, 49, 145; communities in, 96, 145, 150; cycles of use and return in, 158, 176; *see also* Conservation; Ecology; Environment
Nebraska, 115, 123
New Deal, 128

INDEX

New England, 40, 42; industrialization of, 31–32; maple forests in, 97
New Mexico, 144, 148
New Orleans: and development of pollution-free transportation, 175; sewage problem in, 61
New York City, 54–57, 59, 60–61, 69, 71, 94; Central Park in, and Olmsted, 62–67, 68, 165; epidemics in, 57, 60–61; slums in, 56; sweatshops in, 88
New York State, 105; forests of, 103
Niagara Falls, 67
Nitrates: in explosives, 116; in fertilizers, 117
Nitrogen, 158
Norris, George W., 114–29, 131, 132, 134; cheap electric power advocated by, 120; in Congress, 115, 117, 118, 122–23, 127–28; and Muscle Shoals, 116–23 *passim*, 126; and Roosevelt, Franklin D., 126, 127, 128; and Teapot Dome, 118, 119; and TVA, 128, 131, 132
Norris, Tennessee, 133
Norris Dam, 129–30, 133
North Carolina, 99
Norton, Charles Eliot, 63

Nuclear-bomb testing, 163
Nuclear power, 134

Ocean: food chains of, 158; Rachel Carson's study of, 157, 158; radioactive wastes dumped into, 164
Ohio, 114
Ohio River, 19, 121, 130
Oklahoma, 62, 119
Olmsted, Frederick Law, 54, 55–71, 174; and Central Park, 63–67, 68, 165; and "city beautiful" movement, 68; as editor of *Nation*, 67; as head of U.S. Sanitary Commission, 67; as landscape architect, 68; "Riverside" planned by, 70; as Staten Island farmer, 58–59; travels of, 58, 59–60, 62, 67
Omaha, 129
Origin of Species (Darwin), 46
Ottauquechee River, 39
Oxygen: dispensed by Japanese vending machines, 171; essential to life, 158

Paducah, Kentucky, 130
Passenger pigeons, extinction of, 79
Peattie, Donald Culross, quoted, 94
Pennsylvania, 94

Peregrine falcon, destroyed by DDT, 165
Pesticides, 160, 161, 171; dangers in use of, 162
Philadelphia, 14, 17
Pinchot, Gifford, 94–111, 134, 165, 176; European forestry studied by, 95; and Muir, 101; rangers organized by, 107–108; and Roosevelt, Theodore, 102–106 passim, 109, 110, 111; as United States Forester, 102, 104; in West, 95–97
Pittsburgh, 129, 157; coal mines near, 88; smoke problem in, 61, 156
Plankton, 158
Plants, green, 158
Pollution, environmental, 20, 41, 47, 48, 70, 89, 119, 164, 169–77 passim
Population, rising, concern about, 89, 163
Predators, as essential part of living community, 145
Progressive movement, 109

Radioactive fallout, 163, 164
Railroads, America changed by, 61
Rangers, organized by Pinchot, 107–108
Recycling of wastes, 175, 176

Red Cross, American, 67
Redwoods, California, 165
Reform, during Theodore Roosevelt period, 108–109
Rivers, pollution of, 20, 47, 89, 119, 175
Rockets, space, 134
Rocky Mountains, 95
Ronaldson (ship), 58
Roosevelt, Franklin D., 126–28, 132, 134; and New Deal, 128; and Norris, 126, 127, 128
Roosevelt, Theodore, 102–106 passim, 108, 115, 134; and Pinchot, 102–106 passim, 109, 110, 111; and Progressive movement, 109; public domain protected by, 106, 107, 115; Tennis Cabinet of, 106

St. Louis: slums in, 61; tanneries in, 88
San Francisco, 84, 90, 125, 175
Sand County Almanac, A (Leopold), 150
Science, resources of, for saving environment, 49, 173
Sea, *see* Ocean
Sequoia, giant, 86
Sewage disposal, 71, 169
Sheep, 77, 105
Shelley, Percy Bysshe, quoted, 54

INDEX

Sierra Club, 90
Sierra Nevada, the, 85, 87, 90, 165
Silent Spring (Carson), 155, 162, 164, 165
Smithsonian Institution, 45
Smog, 170
Snake Lake, 175
Soil: conditioned with waste matter and garbage, 134; erosion of, 105, 108, 122
South, the, 96, 104
Southwest, the, 144, 146
Soviet Union, 123
Space rockets, 134
Springdale, Pennsylvania, 155, 156
Steelmaking, 89, 156
Stock-market crash (1929), 124
Strip mining, 119
Strontium-90, 163
Suburbs, planned, 69–70
Sulfur fumes, vegetation destroyed by, 122

Teapot Dome, 118, 119
Technology, 173; hidden hazards of, 172
Telegraph, America changed by, 61
Tellico, Tennessee, 133
Tennessee, 123, 124
Tennessee River, 116, 120, 121, 128, 129, 130

Tennessee Valley Authority (TVA), 128–34 *passim*
Texas, 62, 89
Thoreau, Henry David, 21, 25–30, 32, 33–35, 165, 174, 175; and explosion of powder mill, 34–35; quoted, 31, 33–34; at Walden Pond, 30–31, 34
Timberlands, *see* Forests
Transportation systems, pollution-free, 175
Twain, Mark, 88
Tweed, William Marcy, 66
Typhoid fever, 57, 61

Union Pacific Railroad, 85

Vanderbilt family, 100
Vaux, Calvert, 64
Vermont, 35, 46; soil exhausted in, 45
Virginia, 133

Walden (Thoreau), 35
Walden Pond, 30–31, 34
Washington, Booker T., 88
Washington, D.C., 89, 102, 104, 105, 115, 122, 127, 131, 174
Water pollution, 20, 41, 47, 70, 89, 119, 164, 170, 175
Webster, Daniel, 67
West, the, 85, 90, 91, 95, 104, 105, 108, 147

Wilderness: protection of, 90, 146, 147–48; and Sierra Club, 90
Wilderness Act, 165
Wilderness Society, 148
Wildlife, 140, 141, 142, 162
Wilson Dam, 118, 126
Wisconsin, 78, 139, 147, 151, 175; University of, 148
Wisconsin River, 149
Wolves, hunting of, 144
Woodlands, *see* Forests
Woodstock, Vermont, 39, 40, 41
Wordsworth, William, quoted, 38

Yellow fever, 60
Yosemite National Park, 67